10663632

Bethlehem Road

Bethlehem Road

by Nancy Crowe

Odd Girls Press, Anaheim, CA

Copyright © 2002 Nancy Crowe

Original art and cover design by Lucy Tabcum, copyright 2002, all
rights reserved. Email: <artbylucy@hotmail.com>

All rights reserved. No part of this work may be reproduced in any
form, except for the quotation of brief passages in reviews, without prior
written permission from Odd Girls Press, P O Box 2157, Anaheim, CA
92814-0157, 800-821-0632, email: publisher@OddGirlsPress.com

This is a work of fiction. Names, characters, and incidents are either
the products of the author's imagination or are used fictitiously. Any
resemblance to actual events or locales or persons, living or dead, is
entirely coincidental.

First edition, 2002

10 9 8 7 6 5 4 3 2 1

Library of Congress Control Number: 2001094994

Crowe, Nancy, 1967—
Bethlehem Road : a novel / Nancy Crowe
p. 190   cm.
ISBN (trade paper): 1-887237-00-3

Lesbians — Fiction.
Intergenerational relations — Fiction.
San Francisco (Calif.) — Fiction.
Middle West — Fiction.

Dedication

For Mom and Kathy and in loving memory of
Dad and Ginny

Acknowledgments

Heartfelt thanks go to Johanna Bos and Cathy Miller for
their encouragement many drafts ago; to Margaret
Gillon and Katherine Forrest for their invaluable
professional guidance; and, as always,
to my family and friends for
their enduring love
and support.

Contents

Sojourn

Chapter One

Ruth glanced in the rearview mirror to make sure the trailer was still attached. The last thing she or Naomi needed was for something else to come loose. But it would be a change to be the ones speeding away instead of being left like turtles in traffic.

Naomi had been Ruth's mother-in-law, although she would probably die before admitting it. The man who had helped them hook up the trailer at the rental station had given them both the once-over, as if he was trying to figure out whether the tiny blonde sixty-something Naomi could be any relation to Ruth, forty years younger and several inches taller. Ruth wore hiking boots and had multiple piercings, and blunt-cut hair that covered the spectrum of brown to blonde. Naomi's pink cotton blouse had dainty lace trim. They shared none of the same features or mannerisms, except for arms folded in resigned boredom. They shared nothing, really, except Naomi's daughter, Marina, who had discarded them both.

Naomi had rented the biggest trailer her small car could handle to haul home what was left of her ten years in San Francisco. It bobbed behind them as Naomi pressed a terry-cloth-clad foot — she hadn't changed out of her house slippers — to the accelerator and passed an even slower-moving sedan on the interstate. She gripped the steering wheel as if it were a ladder from which she might fall.

She had not asked Ruth, a native of the city she had so feared and despised, to help her pack. She had not asked Ruth to study the atlas and determine where one road connected with another. She had not, for that matter, asked Ruth to accompany her on the drive to Indiana. Ruth had anyway.

Ruth stretched her long legs out in front of her; they were tanned beneath the khaki shorts and the thick socks that kept her boots from chafing. The trip would seem twice as long if Naomi didn't start complaining about the roads or the other drivers, speculating on how far they should drive that night, or voicing whatever other thoughts charged through her mind. Ruth reminded herself that Naomi could not be expected to act like herself after what she'd just been through, and her silence might be welcome on this long road trip. Ruth had lived with Marina, Naomi's firstborn, for two years, and Marina often got so tired of her mother's chatter that she would not talk to Ruth for hours after they'd spent time with Naomi.

Ruth twisted around to look at the trailer again. The San Francisco skyline faded into the hazy sky behind it, like a place they had passed through and promptly forgotten.

❧

They stopped to eat somewhere near Reno, in a diner with the requisite colorless tile floor, gold-speckled tabletops, and patrons whose heads turned toward the two women who came through the door and sat in a booth by the window. Ruth picked up a menu and pretended to ignore the eyes that swept over the six earrings and one cuff in her right ear, and the little gold eyebrow ring. The eyes held the same suspicion, then disapproval, as Naomi's had when she first met Ruth. That was all right; Ruth didn't want to look like anyone else, especially these people in their plaid and polyester. The jewelry alone set her apart in most settings, if nothing else did.

The patrons' scrutiny shifted to Naomi in her wrinkled blouse, black gabardine slacks that made a light swishing sound when she walked or crossed her matchstick-thin legs, and maroon house slippers. According to the pictures Marina had kept on her bookcase, Naomi's hair had once been some kind of brown. Now the gray had declared a truce with a wash of bleached blonde that framed a round, moderately lined face in haphazard waves. People always smiled and said they didn't believe she was nearing seventy, but today they would. Today the glances toward Naomi, particularly from older patrons, turned sympathetic before they were politely averted.

"What's the weather like in Indiana at this time of year?" Ruth asked after a few minutes of silence. Certainly they could find something to talk about. She'd start with something easy.

Naomi took a swallow of iced tea. "May's usually nice. Then it'll get hot and sticky."

More silence. So much for the weather. "Who else in your family is still there besides your cousin?"

"No one, except for her daughter."

Ruth waited, fiddling with one of her earrings. She would have expected at least a sentence or two on the year the crops nearly died during a heat wave or how Naomi used to cool off in an eccentric neighbor's pond. Or about the summer she and her younger brother and sisters went to live with an aunt while her parents went on the road during the Depression, taking whatever work they could find. Their trek had ended when Naomi's father, wasted on bad whiskey, drove an orchard owner's car into the lake. Such stories had always bubbled forth from Naomi like a spring after a rain, but now she seemed more interested in pushing the cottage cheese around on her plate.

Naomi took another drink of iced tea and briefly met her

eyes, looking at Ruth the way Marina had when she was trying to make up her mind about something and didn't want to show her hand.

At first glance, there wasn't much physical resemblance between Naomi and Marina, who had inherited her volleyball-player height from her father. Marina's hair was long, dark, and usually pulled back to be out of her way; Naomi was forever trying to talk her into having it cut or getting a permanent wave. But they shared the same light blue eyes and a solidity about the nose and mouth, and a certain set to the chin or probing gaze would leave no doubt that they were mother and daughter. Ruth's stomach knotted up. She couldn't afford to think about Marina now.

"I'll drive," Ruth said in the parking lot.

"Oh, that's all right, I'll —"

"We said we'd switch off driving, remember?" Ruth held out her hand.

Naomi stopped in the middle of the lot and scanned the faded pavement and fuzzy yellow lines as if she'd dropped something. After a pickup truck with a failing muffler edged past, she dug into her big straw purse and handed over the keys on a ring with a silver cross.

Ruth adjusted the driver's seat and mirrors, then sat up straight and eased the car and trailer back onto the interstate, waiting fruitlessly for Naomi to tell her to brake sooner or get into the other lane. In the same way, Naomi had hovered near the door of her small apartment on Estancia Boulevard, offering little input as Ruth and the neighbor's husky teenage grandson loaded most of her things into the trailer and car. A Naomi without a better way to do something was not Naomi.

Always, Naomi took the lead, with Marina following behind her and Ruth following behind Marina like a line of baby partridges.

It was not a new formation. Marina had told Ruth about

14   NANCY CROWE

her senior year in high school, when she failed to come up with a date for the prom. She had already planned an evening out with a few volleyball teammates, but Naomi made a couple of phone calls. Within twenty-four hours, she had a date (the son of a friend at church), dress (secondhand, but it would probably fit), and corsage (why leave choosing the right flowers to a teenage boy?) lined up for her daughter. Marina had screamed her outrage and told her mother never, ever to do such a thing again — that she was no one's puppet, least of all Naomi's. A two-day standoff ensued, but when the big night rolled around, there was Marina in the hotel ballroom with a bunch of flowers the size of a funeral spray pinned to her shoulder. When Marina's younger sister, Cara, let it slip that she and her husband were trying to have a baby, Naomi sat her down in the kitchen. Marina and Ruth had been watching television in the next room, but they got up and left when Naomi began advising a red-faced Cara on what positions she and Oliver should assume in order to conceive a boy. A short time later, Naomi took some of Marina's savings — her name had been on the account since Marina opened it in high school — and invested them in some stock or other she'd heard about at church. It was a sure thing, Naomi insisted, and Marina could buy some pretty new clothes with the money she'd make. Marina did not wait around for the dividends. She withdrew all that was left of her bank account and opened a new one in her name only, but she did not tell Naomi what she had done.

Sometimes Naomi dropped by their apartment before Marina came home from work, and Ruth could forget about grading papers or whatever else she might be doing. She would sit on the futon while Naomi plopped herself into the nearest chair, kicked off her laced-up leather sneakers, and launched into a commentary about the day's news from Washington, her new associate pastor's latest gaffe or insult (the man could do no right), or her frustration when Cara wouldn't say much about her visits to the fertility specialist, "the one with the

Spanish name." After all, they didn't have these fancy doctors when Naomi had had to wait months, then years and more years, to get pregnant.

Naomi occasionally asked about Ruth's work, and Ruth would read aloud parts of her students' essays, from the profound to the pathetic. When Marina walked through the door, Ruth would look at the clock and be shocked to find that an hour or two had passed. There was something about Naomi that kept everything around her alive, in motion, and even ridiculously funny.

Once, as they walked in search of a new Thai restaurant in Sausalito, Naomi, Marina, and Ruth passed a middle-aged man with one hand full of leaflets and the other lifted in either praise or warning. "Ladies, I'd like to talk to you about the Lord Jesus Christ."

Naomi had slowed down. "Oh? He talk to you lately?"

"I don't know what to do with her sometimes," Marina had said in a low voice to Ruth, who tried not to laugh out loud.

The man had looked at Naomi soberly. "Ma'am, are you saved?"

"Honey, at my age the best I can hope for is well-preserved, but you have a nice day just the same. Let's go, girls."

It was a story Ruth loved to tell if anyone commented on how much they hung out with Marina's mother, with whom Ruth had spent more time than her own mother over the last two years.

The mountains' shadows stretched as the sun slipped behind them. Ruth looked at the clock on the dashboard, which hadn't displayed the right time in months, and then at her watch. Three more hours, maybe two, and they'd stop for the night.

NANCY CROWE

Naomi must have felt it first — the muffled bang followed by the painful scrape of wheel rim against asphalt, cushioned only by a layer of useless rubber. "Oh, hell. Pull over!" Ruth was already guiding the car onto the shoulder and making sure the trailer wasn't sticking out onto the interstate.

Naomi jumped out and bent to look at the right front tire. "What'd you run over?" she demanded.

Ruth, too, bent to peer at the tire. Her hair swung forward and she pushed it back, wondering if, even at a moment like this, Naomi would offer to cut bangs for her again. She crouched to look at it from the other side, Naomi looking over her shoulder. After a minute or so of study, Ruth determined that the tire was, indeed, flat.

"You must've hit a nail or something." Naomi looked back down the road as if she could spot the offending object.

"I don't see anything."

"You sure don't. I guess you weren't watching where you were going."

Ruth took a deep breath. "I mean, I don't see anything in the tire that would have punctured it." She looked at Naomi, who kicked at some gravel with the toe of her house slipper. "Got any tools?" Naomi shook her head, and Ruth wondered why she had asked. Even if she had the proper tools, she had no idea how to change a tire. She'd watched a college girl-friend do so once, but that was a few years and several girl-friends ago. "Do you have one of those Call Police banners to put in the windshield?"

"I had two, but I gave one to Marina and the other to Cara." Her daughters' names were almost drowned in a truck's tailwind.

Ruth looked up and down the interstate. They were miles from the nearest exit and the sun was sinking fast. "I guess I'll turn the flashers on, then."

"Oh, you want to kill the battery too? That'll just top everything right off, now, won't it?" Naomi paced along the shoulder.

Ruth put her hands on her hips. "Do you have a better idea?"

Naomi whirled around. "As a matter of fact, I do. If we don't get killed out here, I'm putting you on a bus back to San Francisco." She turned away again.

"What?" Ruth yelled into the wind.

"You think I don't know why Marina moved to Seattle?"

Ruth's heart tumbled onto the highway. "What do you mean?"

"I never said a goddamn word about Marina living with you. Not one goddamn word!" Naomi, her face as pink as the sunburn she didn't have, jabbed a bony finger at Ruth. "But the only way she could get free of you was to pick up and move six hundred and whatever miles away to a strange town." Two more semis roared past.

Naomi knew. Ruth had always known she did, even though Marina had insisted her mother would never know. "She didn't exactly ask you to keep in touch, either, did she?" Ruth fired back.

Naomi looked at Ruth as if she had picked up a chunk of highway and hurled it straight for her head. She moved a step closer to the guard rail meant to prevent cars, but not humans, from falling down the rocky slope.

"Look, I…" Ruth tried to steady her breathing. "I know this is a hard time… it is for me, too, and I don't think —"

"Don't give me that shit," Naomi shouted over the traffic. "*You* lose your only grandchild and have both your girls leave town without so much as a wave, and then you can tell me about hard times!"

Ruth leaned against the car, arms folded, eyes and lips tightly closed. Naomi kept pacing along the rough gravel shoulder in her slippers. Ruth knew they should get back into the car and lock the doors, but the last place she wanted to be was in a small, closed space with Naomi.

They waited in silence as cars and trucks shot past, drivers and passengers glancing uninterestedly at them as they would at any other road debris. The sun had all but disappeared behind two mountains, leaving a surreal orange glow in its wake.

This is America, Ruth's mother used to say on the trips the family took when Ruth was a child, although they never ventured so far from San Francisco by car. They were young professionals on the open road, cut loose from the City and fancying themselves explorers in jeans and golf shirts. Her mother loved stopping at roadside fruit stands and antique shops; she picked through wooden baskets of squash and grapefruit while the wind whipped at the chestnut hair she almost always kept in a neat pageboy. Her father would stroll up and down rows of souvenirs and lawn ornaments, hands in the pockets of the green windbreaker he only wore on vacations. He had always wanted a garden full of gnomes, but Ruth couldn't remember him ever buying one. A fidgety child, she didn't care where they stopped as long as they didn't stay too long. She would watch her parents browse and wonder how much further they had to travel.

Naomi opened a rear door and reached into the back seat. "Damn cops are probably sitting in a doughnut shop." She pulled out a pink sweater which had once been fuzzy and put it on. She looked at Ruth, crumpled against the right front fender. "If one ever shows up, we'll have him drop you at the nearest bus station."

"Why?" Ruth kept her tone as even as she could and still be heard.

"Your folks are right there in town and you hardly ever see them. You ought to go back and spend some time with your own mom."

"My mom?" Ruth turned to look at her. "You know she can't be bothered with me."

Naomi hesitated. "Well, this isn't any kind of vacation for

you, and a one-way ticket from Indiana'll cost an arm and a leg."

"It's not a problem," Ruth said. "I said I'd drive back with you to your family, and I will."

"Family?" Naomi snorted. "My cousin Belinda's the only family I've got left, and I haven't seen her in more than ten years. You don't know her or anyone else in that part of the country. Why the hell do you want to go with me?"

Ruth brushed some dust from the side-view mirror. She imagined Naomi ten years ago, newly arrived from Indiana with her husband and daughters, the loyal wife and mother gasping and bracing herself as the car crested one San Francisco hill after another. Those variations in the earth's surface could sneak up on you, even if you were a native who supposedly knew the territory.

Naomi turned away, mumbling something Ruth couldn't understand, but she'd heard enough anyway. "Naomi, I packed up your life and stuffed it into that goddamn trailer and got you this far, and I'm not letting you drive all the way to Indiana by yourself!" Ruth realized she'd gone from shouting to yelling, and that it was probably the first time she'd called Marina's mother by name. "So knock off this shit about sending me back. Understand?"

Neither of them moved. Naomi's eyes burned through the thickening dusk. Ruth's pulse raced, and collapsing right there on the interstate seemed not only possible but wise.

Naomi got back into the car on the passenger's side, closed the door, and pulled her sweater around her. She did not speak to Ruth when the trooper pulled up a few minutes later, while they waited for the tire to be fixed, or when they checked into a motor inn across from the garage because there was no use going any further that night.

And the two of them went on, through the mountains toward the East.

Chapter Two

Naomi steered the car down a ruler-straight stretch of Nebraska interstate. The man on the radio said the area had been hit by a tornado two days ago, but it looked untouched. Maybe there wasn't much a tornado could do to some places; life had flattened them already. Gas stations, hotels, factories, shopping centers, and weathered farmhouses and barns surfaced along the road like blips on a heart monitor. If one got burned down or leveled by a storm, there'd be another a few miles down the road.

They passed another series of green and blue signs, with Ruth hunched over the road atlas. "It looks like this might be the last rest stop for a while."

Naomi didn't remember much about the drive ten years ago on the other side of the highway, from Indiana to California, but she'd been scared so bad she could hardly stay in the car. The recession had all but shut down the factory, and Ed had decided to bolt before he got laid off. Some fellow he'd worked with years ago had some kind of human resource consulting business starting up out in San Francisco and needed a partner. Naomi started praying. There were earthquakes out there; without warning, the ground could come right out from under you and swallow you up. What's more, she knew what kind of people lived in and swarmed toward San Francisco.

Naomi and Ed promised the girls and their extended families that they would come back and visit, but they never did. Flying was too frightening for Naomi and too expensive for Ed, and there were always plenty of reasons not to make that road trip to Indiana.

The car's right wheels dropped onto the shoulder, and Ruth jumped. "Whoops," Naomi muttered, jerking the car back into the lane. Ruth looked at her with one eyebrow raised and the other furrowed. How did she do that, Naomi wondered. Naomi kept telling her those eyebrows could use some plucking so that she'd have a nice clean arch over each eye, but she never did it. From the beginning, her eyes had unnerved Naomi. They could be green or brown, depending on the light and what she wore, and they never missed a thing. She always looked Naomi right in the eye when she talked to her, unless something distracted or bothered her, like when Naomi offered to cut her hair or pluck her eyebrows. Or when Naomi came by the apartment the day after Marina left — Ruth wouldn't hardly look at her then. Today Ruth's eyes were green as leaves after the rain.

Naomi pushed the eject button to stop the tape, one of those girl singers Ruth liked. No wonder she couldn't concentrate on her driving. She scanned the dial until she heard a good country tune and left it there. What you listened to made a difference in how you felt. Cara had made her husband bring their little portable stereo to the hospital and play harpy New Age music while she was giving birth, but it must not have helped because she asked Naomi to leave after a couple of strong contractions. Naomi swore she wouldn't go back into that room even if Cara cried for her, but then that Nazi of a nurse came and got her.

When she first saw her grandson, just minutes after he

NANCY CROWE

was born, Naomi had forgotten all about Cara. This tiny boy child would be the first in the family to show what a man ought to be, and Naomi hoped to God she'd live long enough to see it. When you didn't get to be a mother until you were forty, any time you got as a grandmother was a bonus.

She'd walked back and forth across the room with Evan, humming the first tune that came into her mind, a TV jingle for floor wax. Ed would be sorry he missed out on this, and it served him right. He'd stuck with her through more than thirty years of want: they wanted a nice wedding, they wanted a house, they wanted a better job for Ed, and they desperately wanted children. Before all that, they wanted each other, and Naomi thought that would carry them through the other wants. Then, when he had two beautiful daughters, he decided he didn't want any of them and moved to Los Angeles with that woman at the bank who'd tried to help him rescue the business. He'd thrown in a few bucks for the girls' college expenses and kept in touch when he felt like it, but other than that he was gone.

She'd half hoped Cara would have twins or triplets; that sometimes happened when you took fertility drugs. But it turned out that one grandchild was about all she could handle. She had forgotten about the crying that filled her ears and head, the diapers, the trips to the pediatrician, and the worrying. Cara kept saying she and Oliver could handle the dirty work, that Naomi just needed to cuddle and admire him, but they didn't know what the hell they were doing. She never had believed in breastfeeding, but Cara insisted. Then they let Evan get a diaper rash a couple of times. It was worth battling that crazy California traffic to go down to San Jose to sit on Cara and Oliver's lumpy couch for hours on end and hold him, look at him, and know that he was real.

Fertility drugs or no, she'd figured Cara would have another baby or two before Marina gave her grandchildren. Cara had always been easier. She had her father's fair hair and carefree smile and looked like a California girl before they ever got there. Even as a baby she was happy just to sit in one of those doorway swings, giddy and content. Marina got her height from her father, but fortunately that was about all. She took longer to make up her mind, and you never could tell what the result might be. She was particular, but if she could share her apartment with that Ruth Greene for two years, surely she could find a halfway decent husband. Part of Marina's problem was that godforsaken shelter where she helped those poor girls whose son-of-a-bitch husbands beat them so bad they couldn't hardly tell in from out. Ed never laid a hand on Naomi or the girls, but he was a son-of-a-bitch just the same. If Marina insisted on going to a church other than Naomi's, which she'd started doing some years ago, Naomi hoped she'd at least find a young man worth her time. So far, she hadn't. Naomi had introduced her to sons and nephews of friends at her own church; one was a lawyer, one was a youth pastor, and a couple more worked with computers and had to be making good money. Nothing clicked.

Ruth was nice enough, if you could look past all that hardware in her ear — and in her eyebrow, for heaven's sake, and that blunt-cut, not-quite-brown-or-blonde hair falling in front of her face. And those boots. They looked like something Naomi's daddy had worn on the farm. She reminded Naomi of a colt, long-legged and graceful but not entirely sure of itself. She'd always been polite to Naomi, and that was something these days, especially in San Francisco. At first Naomi thought Ruth was some sort of pagan; she wore crystals that were supposed to do things like boost energy and increase openness to truth. Then Ruth started going to church with Marina, and Naomi prayed that Marina's influence in that department would cancel out whatever other influence Ruth was having on Marina.

Way before they moved to San Francisco, Naomi had decided that as long as she kept an eye on her girls, they'd be all

NANCY CROWE

right. A mother was the most important influence a daughter would ever have, and that was only fair. Naomi had discovered, when Marina was born, that motherhood was not something a woman did. It wasn't even something she was given, although people talked about being blessed with children. It was a force that took over. Once that tiny body was ripped from hers, nothing looked or felt the same. Cars became careening deadly weapons, a sneeze meant pneumonia, and every stranger was a molester or murderer. There, between all of that and your baby, you stood — alone.

Naomi glanced sideways, trying to keep the wheels in line with the road. Those eyes of Ruth's seemed to set nowhere, and she absently tucked a strand of hair that might be called golden behind her left ear. What on earth did Ruth's mother think about the way she looked? Then again, Ruth's mother was probably a good twenty years younger than Naomi. Since the day she found out she was pregnant with Marina, Naomi had wondered about the difference being twenty years younger might make.

"I'm sick of restaurants," Ruth announced, exiting the interstate as dinnertime approached in Iowa or wherever they were. She'd moved the seat back, adjusted the sun visor and tilted the rearview mirror, the way she did every time she took the wheel, and Naomi would have to change it all back again.

She went into a convenience store while Naomi waited, a passenger in her own car. Twenty-four miles later, they were dining at a rest stop picnic table.

Naomi nibbled a potato chip from a bag Ruth had thrown into the back seat in San Francisco while Ruth assembled ham, cheese, mayonnaise, and bread almost in a single motion and handed it to her on a napkin. She had helped Naomi and Marina out in the kitchen plenty of times, but Naomi had seen nothing like this.

"How'd you do that so quick?" Naomi turned the sandwich this way and that, inspecting it.

Ruth popped open a plastic container and spread dressing from a foil packet onto her salad. She didn't eat meat. The first time Marina brought her over for dinner, she wouldn't eat the pot roast Naomi had cooked. "I worked in the cafeteria in college," Ruth said. "I lasted only about two months, but I learned how to make a sandwich in nothing flat."

"What a talent," Naomi mumbled.

They sat in the late spring breeze, the funny-looking girl and the dried-up old broad, listening to the semis groan by. Naomi ate more than she had since they'd set out.

NANCY CROWE

Chapter Three

New Bethlehem, Indiana
A Small Town with a Big Future

So a billboard proclaimed as the highway became Main Street. Through the day's dying light, Ruth read the signs — car wash signs, restaurant signs, everything. About one in three contained a misspelling. On almost every corner a sign pointed the way to this church or that one, and another billboard behind a Dairy Queen declared the correctness of a nationally syndicated conservative talk-radio host. A car wash marquee bore the warning, Jesus: Don't Leave Earth Without Him.

Naomi and Ruth had just come through rolling green hills with a lone cabin here and there and vistas suddenly opening through the trees as they rounded a curve. Ruth wished they could have passed this way in broad daylight. The dusk covering New Bethlehem hid much of its terrain, but the place looked as flat as cardboard and about as interesting.

A solid limestone courthouse sat in the middle of the town square, which consisted of several shops with names like The Posy Patch, a mammoth Baptist church, an attorney's office or two, a diner with paint peeling around the windowsills and half its sign burned out, and some kind of agricultural office. The streaks of sunset had barely faded from the sky, but hardly a soul was in sight except for a pack of teenagers edging around a corner, and a shuffling older fellow who was probably the town drunk. Ruth had heard the jokes about places where the sidewalks got rolled up at night and turned to Naomi to say something, then thought better of it.

Naomi drove as if she had not been gone for ten years and did not have to think about new landmarks. Ruth had hoped Naomi might point out where she and her family had lived, their church, where Marina went to school. Or the factory — Naomi had said everyone in town either worked there or was married to someone who did. But Naomi was as silent in her home town as she had been on most of the trip. Perhaps she felt no need to name anything or explain its significance, at least not to Ruth.

Naomi's cousin owned a rather large, two-story brick house a couple of blocks from the square, on a street with old houses and even older trees. A child's pale blue bicycle sprawled on the front porch next to a set of worn patio furniture and scattered gardening tools. As far as Ruth knew, Naomi had phoned her cousin and said only that she was coming home — nothing about another person coming along for the ride. Now Ruth wondered how, indeed, Naomi would explain her presence to whomever opened the door. By the time they reached the doorstep with their bags, she didn't care about that or anything else except being out of that car for a while. When the door opened, Naomi said with a tight smile, "This is Ruth, a friend of Marina's. She's helping an old lady across the country."

Belinda was somewhere in the neighborhood of fifty, slender like Naomi but taller; with collar-length dark hair streaked with gray, and intelligent blue eyes. She wore jeans and a striped blouse and held a pair of wire-rimmed glasses in one hand, as if she had been reading and had taken them off to

NANCY CROWE

answer the door. Ruth tried to place her among the faces in Naomi's photos, but could not, nor could she recall anything about Belinda from Naomi's ramblings other than that she was a doctor, the smart one in the family.

She shook Ruth's hand with a warm, firm grasp, not seeming at all surprised that a stranger had accompanied her cousin from the West Coast. "Ruth, welcome."

It was a simple greeting, but Ruth felt some of the tension leave her neck and shoulders. She hauled their suitcases into the entry hall, listening politely as Naomi answered the usual how-was-your-trip questions.

Through a dining room with an arched, wide entry she could see a kitchen full of cooking gadgets and a refrigerator door plastered with art such as only a child could create. Books, papers, and file folders covered one end of the dining room table as if it served as a desk but could be a bona fide eating area at a moment's notice. A television set mumbled from the living room, straight back from the entry hall.

Judging from the woodwork, hardwood floors, and high ceilings, Ruth thought the house must be at least eighty years old. It lacked the high-heeled stance of some San Francisco houses of the same era; this house sat like a favorite aunt in a hand-carved rocking chair. The place had settled into its inhabitants, as well as the other way around. Or inhabitant, she guessed. From what little Naomi had said, Belinda lived alone.

She almost didn't hear Belinda ask if they wanted to go to church with her the next morning.

"Is tomorrow Sunday?" Ruth asked absently. She thought they'd passed Sunday two time zones ago.

"Reckon so," Naomi said with a sigh. "Nope. I got nothing to say to the Lord." Her mouth, which hadn't seen its usual coral lipstick in weeks, flattened. She shouldered her overnight bag and trudged upstairs, pulling herself up by the oak banister.

Belinda and Ruth looked after her in silence. Was this Naomi? The same woman who, the first time she met Ruth, asked if she went to church? The woman who, on the Thanksgiving Ruth had spent with Marina, thanked God for each person at the table?

Ruth felt the urge to smile and say something, anything to fill the space, or to apologetically whisper that Naomi was tired and would feel more sociable in the morning. But she was on Naomi's turf. Ruth was the one who had left the comfort of her native city and traveled two thousand miles to a place and people she did not know. And yet another member of this family had asked her to go to church.

Toto, we're not in San Francisco anymore. Ruth almost said it out loud. She would have to listen to more platitudes about love, community, and perseverance in a part of the country where such piety might be delivered with a fiery sting. Or she could spend the morning with Naomi.

Ruth turned back to Belinda. "Sure." She managed a smile.

"Great. But if you need to get some extra rest like Naomi, don't feel obligated," Belinda said. She had a quiet voice, one that must be reassuring to patients. She stood with her hands folded and looked at Ruth with such kindness that she thought she might burst into tears.

"All right. I… hope I'm not imposing on you in any way." Ruth's gaze dropped from Belinda's friendly smile to the fringed, blue-patterned rug in the entry hall.

"Not at all. I'm glad Naomi didn't try to make that trip by herself," Belinda said. "This house has plenty of room — sometimes I wonder why I don't sell it to a family with eight kids." She chuckled. "I'm going to put you in one of the front rooms. It'll be a little cooler in there if we get a hot spell."

Ruth followed her up the stairs and down a hallway that creaked under their feet. They passed a closed door with a strip of light showing underneath and no sound from within. "Naomi must've taken Eliza's old room," Belinda whispered.

NANCY CROWE

"How about this?"

The next room was decorated in airy eggshell tones, with an office-style metal desk and swivel chair, a squat chest of drawers, a few boxes, and a twin bed in the corner. A large teddy bear wearing an old striped tie reclined against the pillow. "This is my sometime-guest room and rest-of-the-time catch-all," Belinda said. "Anything I don't know quite what to do with goes in here." Then, obviously realizing what she had said, she raked her fingers through her hair, which was more gray than dark near her forehead and looked like fine silk. "Oh — I didn't mean... oh, shoot. Can I get you something to eat? Some tea?"

Ruth smiled, almost too tired to note the color in her hostess's cheeks. "No, thanks. I think I'll just read for a while and go to bed."

Belinda, still red-faced, bid her goodnight, leaving a musky floral scent in her wake.

Ruth helped herself to a clean towel in the bathroom, washed up, and crawled into bed to read. Her eyes scanned the same paragraph several times.

She was in the Midwest, that yawning hole in the middle of the country, in the small town which had been the only home Marina knew until she was sixteen. Tall, athletic Marina, who moved on foot and in conversation like a boxer or tennis player, evaluating, anticipating, stepping one way and then another with quick-footed grace. That mercurial mix of clear-eyed confidence and disarming vulnerability had held Ruth's interest from the moment they met.

Like this room, Ruth's tiny bedroom in San Francisco had more or less been a place to stash whatever was currently unnecessary. Clothes, books, and papers were piled onto the bed. If anyone was coming over, she went in and tidied up just enough to make it look lived in. The other bedroom in the apartment had been, as far as anyone else knew, Marina's alone.

Tell the truth, let's be honest, isn't it true. Such phrases had echoed in Ruth's head since she was old enough to comprehend them, and even when she clashed with her parents she agreed that telling the truth was a fundamental value. Her mother, a civil rights attorney, and her father, a professor of political science, had religiously pursued truth and the decimation of anything that got in its way. You couldn't "let it all hang out" the way people had when pain over Vietnam and murdered hopes for social change were as palpable on the street as in anyone's heart. You could and must walk down the street and look every sniper, street preacher, and chief executive officer in the eye and refuse to pretend to be what you were not.

Emily Dickinson, hiding from the world, had written about telling the truth aslant. It was a step above lying, maybe several steps. Telling the truth, straight up in boldface, was next. It was a step that Emily, with her white dresses, breathless verse and supposed secret longing for her sister-in-law, may never have been able to take. For two years Ruth had hoped that with enough love and encouragement, Marina just might. Marina made no promises, but she had stayed longer than anyone else.

Ruth stared at a watercolor painting hanging over the desk; a sailboat blended muddily into water and sky as if the artist had viewed the scene through a rain-splashed window. Why on earth had she come out here? It had done Naomi no good, and now Ruth was in this woman's spare room for extraneous junk.

Well, she'd done what she set out to do. Naomi was back home, for better or for worse, and Ruth could do nothing else for her. She'd had her change of scenery and might as well figure out a way home. She would get away from this family of women who had no use for her and get on with her life.

What if Naomi decided she didn't want to be in New

NANCY CROWE

Bethlehem, after all? Then she would have little choice but to make the return trip to San Francisco alone. Although the room was warm, Ruth burrowed further under the bedclothes. It wasn't as if anything waited for her in San Francisco. She wouldn't start teaching again for several weeks, the ad agency she occasionally wrote copy for hadn't called in months, and many of her friends were away. Some of them, she was sure, did not yet know about the breakup. There were the bars, where there was plenty of company and enough booze and smoke to make you not care. She didn't have to consult a gay travel guide to guess that there probably was not a gay bar within a hundred miles of this horrid little town, or even a women's softball team. She hated softball anyway.

It didn't matter, though. Wherever she went, she would likely end up as part of someone's clutter, something to be shoved into a catch-all room.

Gleaning

Chapter Four

New Bethlehem Presbyterian Church, one of the many lime-stone buildings in the area, stood on a corner near the other side of the town square, its steeple reaching proudly toward the heavens and yet dwarfed by the Baptist church two blocks over. By the time Belinda and Ruth arrived, the organist had begun the prelude and people in suits and pastel cotton dresses trickled through the heavy wooden double doors into the sanctuary. In good old-time Protestant fashion, this church with its plain white walls, austerely curved arches, and nearly threadbare maroon carpet could hardly be called ornate. Still, it was obvious that some loyal band of pioneer Presbyterians had spent their last dollar to build it more than a century ago.

Everyone wanted to greet Belinda. A family with three redheaded girls came up to her in the parking lot and showered her with hugs and reports of a cleared-up skin condition and how much better the youngest one's sprained wrist felt; she smiled and told the child she was sure that just about every gymnast on the Olympic team had sprained her wrist at one time or another. The elderly man in the plaid sport jacket who welcomed churchgoers in the entryway took Belinda's hand in both of his and thanked her for seeing his wife on such short notice last week, and various women of every age flashed by in the sanctuary with embraces, handshakes, and talk of scheduling appointments soon and getting Belinda's input on the youth group's next mission trip. Through all of this, Ruth foggily heard herself introduced as a friend of Naomi's and shook a few hands. Part of her still dragged across the country, on the move but not quite there. After they sat down in a pew about midway back, she rubbed her eyes; she had put on dress pants and the least wrinkled blouse in her suitcase, but she knew she must look like an unholy mess.

The solid oak pews and pulpit, corners and edges rounded off over many decades, had been finished and polished to a classic sheen. Sunlight beamed through a stained-glass portrayal of Jesus, a few disciples, and a child or two, all fair despite their Middle Eastern origins. The place looked like a smaller, more modest version of Marina's church in San Francisco, the moderate mainline congregation she had joined because it was not her mother's nondenominational megachurch. New Bethlehem Presbyterian had the same appointments of times past, but with more pickup trucks lining the street outside.

A young couple, preceded by a bright-eyed little girl of about seven, filed into Ruth's pew. The child bounded forward, long hair flying, and landed on the cushioned pew next to Belinda with a jarring thud.

"Sarah, settle down," the young woman, presumably the girl's mother, admonished. She was about Ruth's age or a little younger, a bit plump, with curly brown hair and a face right out of a soap commercial.

"Okey-dokey." Sarah grinned from the crook of Belinda's arm.

"Well, I'll be. You're on time," Belinda teased. She introduced Ruth to her daughter, Eliza, and Eliza's husband, Mark, a tall, quiet man with a neatly trimmed beard. Sarah, their daughter, had already slipped past the adults and out the other end of the pew. She was tiny and wiry, with bright blue eyes and a flyaway look, as if at any moment her hair might come loose from the wide pink barrette or her Sunday-best dress could become irretrievably rumpled and she wouldn't notice or care.

"Where's Naomi?" Eliza asked her mother. "Sarah, get back here!" she commanded in a stage whisper.

"She wasn't quite up for it this morning. A little road-weary, I think," Belinda said. "Ruth doesn't wear out as quickly as us older folks do."

Ruth blinked a couple of times. "You'd be surprised."

Every single child who came forward for the children's message was white. Ruth pictured them singing in their little matching robes, a monochromatic choir of angels.

Sarah listened carefully, hunkered down with the other kids and the minister on the chancel steps; she tried to be the first to answer his questions and fidgeted when he called on someone else. She had her grandmother's eyes, and Ruth could imagine her calmly listening to a patient in a few decades.

"She seems like a smart kid," Ruth whispered as the children trooped out of the sanctuary to Sunday school.

"She is. Too smart for her own good sometimes." Belinda's eyes followed her granddaughter. "But she keeps me going."

A few coughs echoed as the congregation, a sea of mostly gray heads, settled in for the sermon. Ruth shifted in the pew. Which would it be: hellfire and brimstone, metaphors about sheep and goats, or brittle quotes from some dead white male theologian?

The Rev. Jim Foster had a fringe of graying hair and a voice surprisingly easy to listen to, given its nasal tone. He read the Bible story of the woman looking for the lost coin and paused to adjust his glasses, a dark, squarish frame style Ruth's father had worn when she was little.

"Ever lose something?" he asked in an unassuming twang. "You had it a minute ago, but where is it now? You look in all the places where it might be, the logical places. When that doesn't work, you start looking in all the illogical places. It seems to have vanished, and that worries your last nerve.

"Imagine how this woman felt — nine silver coins present and accounted for, and one missing in action. Maybe that tenth coin would make the difference between eating and not eating for a day or two. Maybe it would make the difference between paying off a loan and remaining in debt. Anyhow, she had to find it, so she did what my mother used to do when she lost something, or when something got her riled up: She cleaned the devil out of that house."

Chuckles rippled through the sanctuary. Ruth turned to look at Belinda, and her focus suddenly sharpened. All that time in the car with Naomi must have dulled the sixth sense she'd had and cultivated since her early teens, the sense she could not explain even if she tried.

The sermon faded as Ruth pondered the new data. Did Naomi know or suspect anything? Probably not. She had not seen her cousin in years, ample time to forget what she'd never wanted to think about.

"What's missing in your life?" The minister's question drew her attention again. "Do you know what it is? And if you do, are you willing to turn your world upside down in order to find it? And when you do find it, what then? Do you put it in its place and go on about your business, hoping nobody notices, or do you call together your friends and neighbors and say, 'Rejoice with me'?

"You see, God can be like that," he said, draping his arms over the pulpit as if he had done so every Sunday for thirty years, which he probably had. "God is like the woman who knows what she is searching for, and when she finds it — or, I should say, when she finds us — she finds every reason to celebrate. And when we seek God, should we not also celebrate? Wherever we find God — in the logical places, and many of the illogical places, we are found and claimed as

NANCY CROWE

God's people. To God be the glory. Amen."

"Amen," the congregation murmured. Ruth glanced around; certainly someone would rise up and object, or at least look righteously aghast, at the minister's comparison of God to a persistent woman. No one was even scowling. Maybe they hadn't heard.

Eliza, Mark, and Sarah followed them back to the house, and Belinda stirred up a pot of stew she'd prepared earlier.

"I know it's the wrong time of year for stew," Belinda said, drying her hands on her linen skirt, "but when you have all the makings for stew and you don't know who's coming to dinner or when, it seems a shame not to make it."

Eliza sighed. "Mom, you'd have an ice cream social in the middle of January." That sounded like a good idea to Ruth, although she doubted the stew was made with tofu.

Eliza and Belinda had the same slightly turned-up nose and a mouth whose slender lips curved into a smile with little provocation. They both spoke slowly and carefully if they were doing something else at the same time, like adding spices to the stew or adjusting the barrette in Sarah's hair. Mark, who seemed accustomed to occupying himself while his wife and mother-in-law talked, loosened his tie and sat down at the table to read the paper. Sarah sat down with her father and quickly became engrossed in the comics.

Eliza leaned against the counter, which had been extended into a kind of breakfast bar. "So," she began, studying Ruth but trying to do it politely, "how do you know Naomi?"

God, how did anyone know Naomi. "I live — used to live with Marina."

Eliza nodded. "Before she moved to... Texas?"

"Seattle." Belinda went back to sorting through her spice rack. "Cara moved to Texas."

Eliza picked a piece of lint from her dress, a pink and lavender floral print with a wide lace collar. "I haven't heard from either of them in years, but I sent Cara a card... and I asked her to call me when she felt like talking. Collect. I thought maybe we could catch up. But she never called."

"She had a pretty rough time," Ruth said.

"Well, I would think so. And then to go off and leave her husband…" She shook her head. "Does Marina like her new job?"

Ruth shrugged. "I guess so. I haven't talked to her." She saw Belinda glance at her out of the corner of her eye.

"What do you do out in California?" Eliza asked.

"I teach English at a community college. I have the summer off." Ruth, following Eliza's eyes, reached up to adjust an earring and forced herself to pick up a glass instead. "Otherwise, I wouldn't have been able to drive out here with Naomi."

"Well, that worked out pretty good. How long are you here for?"

"I'm not sure. I guess I'd like to help Naomi get settled."

Eliza nodded. "That's really nice of you. Do you have a family?"

"Um… my parents live in San Francisco."

"Any brothers or sisters?"

"No, just me."

Eliza's serious face broke into a smile. "I'm an only child, too."

"We thought we better quit after that one." Belinda nodded in her daughter's direction with a quick wink.

Mark chuckled. "Can't blame you there."

"You two cut it out," Eliza scolded, laughing. She turned back to Ruth. "What does your dad do?"

No one had asked her that since the third grade. "He teaches political science at the university. My mom's an attorney."

"That's kind of neat. So you're not married?"

"No."

"Eliza, are you working for the FBI?" Belinda gently swatted her with a dish towel.

Eliza's cheeks turned pink, and Ruth could almost hear the gears shifting. "Mom, have you seen Sarah's white dress with the blue flowers on it? I went to wash it the other day and couldn't find it."

"It's here," Belinda said. "I can throw it in the laundry if you want."

"Well, I want her to wear it for her school awards program this week," Eliza said. "And if you don't replace that old water heater, you'll be doing all your laundry in cold water." She was already halfway up the stairs, her quick footsteps making the floorboards creak.

"Don't start that again," Belinda called after her. She turned from the stove. "You know, I do believe the world would stop revolving if Eliza wasn't here to take care of every detail."

"Well, somebody's got to do it." Mark rearranged his six-foot frame in the antique oak chair. He caught Ruth's eye and smiled behind his beard, reminding her of Abraham Lincoln in his younger years.

While they waited for the stew to reach just the right temperature, Belinda put a bowl of popcorn — "day-old, but still good" — on the table for nibbling.

"Did you know that only four states grow more corn than Indiana?" Sarah scooped up a handful. "It's the biggest crop in Indiana. Second is soybeans," she added.

"I'm going to put you on *Jeopardy*, Miss Knowitall." Belinda pinched Sarah's nose.

"Okay. I'll win a million dollars and you won't ever have to go to work again." She looked at Mark. "Or you, or Mom."

"Well, I don't know about that." Belinda put silverware on the table. "You might not want us hanging around all day with nothing to do."

Eliza returned with the dress and hung it on the coat rack by the front door.

"Sweetie, did you see Naomi up there?" her mother asked.

"I wonder if I should look in on her."

"No, I didn't. Was she up when you left?" Eliza looked over Mark's shoulder at a Wal-Mart ad. He leafed through the sections and advertisements, careful not to disturb Belinda's place settings.

"No, I think she was still down for the count. Better let her rest. I can always heat up some of this for her later." Belinda turned back to the steaming pot.

Ruth leaned against the kitchen counter, not knowing what to do to help, not comfortable sitting down. She watched Belinda stir the stew, the steam reddening her cheeks.

"Naomi tells me you're a doctor. I'd like to hear more about your practice." Ruth moved a little closer. The concoction smelled just about perfect, although she hadn't had stew in years. It would be difficult to maintain a vegetarian lifestyle in the meat-loving Midwest, and being here was awkward enough already.

Belinda glanced at her and smiled. "What can I say? It's a work in progress."

When they all sat down to eat, Belinda told Ruth how she worked with two other general practitioners from the time she finished medical school until a couple of years after she and Eliza's father divorced. Then she decided it was time to start her own practice.

"I had no idea what she was getting herself into." Eliza salted her stew. "This guy who sold her his house had lived in it for about a hundred years. He couldn't understand how she was going to turn the place into a doctor's office."

"He wasn't quite right in the head, if you ask me," Mark said.

"Well, I don't know about his sanity, but he sure seemed to think I didn't know what I was doing. And I didn't." Belinda chuckled.

"Grandma just got a new computer in her office," Sarah said, "but all it does is keep track of who's paid their bills."

"No games, huh? Bummer," Ruth said. She glanced at her bowl and realized she'd devoured most of her stew — onions, celery, carrots, potatoes, beef, and all.

"We make do." Belinda touched Sarah's cheek on the way to the refrigerator. Ruth wondered if anyone in this family ever sat through a meal. Someone was always getting up for a napkin, more iced tea, a different kind of salad dressing, or something. She had had to take Marina to a restaurant if she wanted her to sit still and eat. She pushed the thought of Marina aside.

Eliza took a roll and neatly folded the napkin over the remaining rolls before passing the basket. "Mom, will Renee even know how to use that computer when she comes back? You got it right before she left."

"Oh, I imagine she'll pick it up pretty quick. Renee's my receptionist," Belinda added to Ruth. "She's taking some time off with her new baby, and Charlene — my nurse — and I are really missing her."

Ruth paused. "I'd be glad to help out while I'm here. I have no medical training or knowledge at all, but I can answer phones and take messages."

Belinda returned to the table. "What a nice offer." A smile spread across her face, and it was directed solely at Ruth. "Sure, come with me tomorrow if you want."

A creak on the stairs issued warning of Naomi's appearance in the doorway, and Ruth pried her eyes away from Belinda. Even after sleeping all night and part of the day, dark half-moons showed under Naomi's eyes. A few halfheartedly-blonde curls were flattened against her head, and the roots needed a touch-up. She had either not found her shoes or not found them worth putting on, and the terry-cloth slippers had picked up some fresh lint.

"Well, look who's up." Belinda rose and went to put an arm around Naomi's shoulders, drawing her into the room. Eliza and Mark were already on their feet.

"It's good to see you again." Eliza had turned shy.

"Eliza." Naomi took her hand. "I haven't seen you since you were a little bitty thing."

She smiled. "This is my husband, Mark... and our little girl, Sarah."

"Ma'am." Mark shook her hand.

Sarah slid off her chair and went to Naomi. "Do you want to see my garden?"

"Sarah, honey, let — Aunt Naomi have some dinner first," Eliza said.

Naomi looked down at Sarah, blinking a couple of times. "Well," she said. "I would love to see your garden." To Belinda, she called over her shoulder, "We'll be right back." The child was already pulling her out the back door.

☙

Ruth had almost finished reading the paper that evening when the doorbell rang.

"Ruth, could you see who that is?" Belinda called from the kitchen. "I've got soapsuds up to my elbows."

"Why didn't you say something? I'll help you with those." Ruth hurried past the kitchen toward the front door.

Out of habit, she peered out the window. Seeing two grandmotherly types, one in a T-shirt with an appliqued teddy bear, she figured it was safe enough to open the door. Both of them looked at Ruth as if they should remember her, but to their chagrin, could not.

"Hello," Teddy Bear Shirt said, eyes sweeping over Ruth again and lingering on each piece of jewelry and the flowing, multicolored blouse Ruth had thrown on over her jeans and a "WimminFest" T-shirt after church and lunch. Her voice was as carefully applied as her light coral lipstick. "You must be..."

"I'm Ruth. Are you looking for Belinda?"

"Well, actually, we heard Naomi Bittner was back in town and thought we'd come by and see for ourselves," the other woman said. She could have been a dancer — lithe, perfect posture, her gray hair swept into a tidy bun. On the left side of her polo shirt, which hung uncertainly on her thin frame, was a leafy Robinson's Nursery logo embroidered in green. "I'm Greta Robinson, an old friend."

"And I'm Lula Masters from next door. It's nice to meet you, Ruth." She held out her hand, palm down. Ruth half expected to see a white glove. Despite the teddy bear T-shirt, simple cotton pants and canvas espadrilles, and despite the fact that she couldn't be more than five foot two, her bearing was that of a duchess. Her hair, still mostly dark, was brushed back from her face in perfect waves.

Ruth shook her hand, then Greta's. The women followed her into the living room, where Naomi slouched in a light blue easy chair, staring at the television. Her face reminded Ruth of the pictures she had seen of Naomi's mother, a frail woman hardened by the early twentieth century Midwest, but without the steely glint of hope that stared into the camera.

"Naomi Sweet, is that you?" Lula burst out before Ruth had a chance to announce them.

Naomi turned her head a fraction of an inch. "Well, Lula, if it's not me, it's some poor idiot who's taken over what's left of me."

"Yup. That's Naomi," Greta said, and they both moved to hug her. Naomi did not get up, but she didn't seem to mind when Lula perched on the sofa and Greta sat on the ottoman next to the chair. She gave them a wan smile, like a patient enduring visiting hours, and sat up a little. They looked like the knots of elderly women Ruth often saw at Marina's church or on the street in San Francisco, banded together against whatever might happen outside their circle.

Ruth slipped into the kitchen. "Some friends of Naomi's are here," she explained.

"I thought I heard Lula and Greta out there." Belinda

wiped the last drops of water from a skillet. "They go all the way back to high school. Before high school, I suppose."

"Wow." Ruth couldn't imagine living that long, let alone maintaining any kind of friendship for so many years. "Point me toward a towel and I'll dry the rest."

Belinda tossed her a dry one from the rack next to the stove. "Did she seem glad to see them?"

"I suppose." Ruth ran the towel over a long serving spoon. "Did you go to high school here?" she asked, knowing she must have but lacking anything better to say.

Belinda smiled. "I sure did. I didn't know too much about life outside New Bethlehem when I went to college and med school, and that was just to the state university where a lot of kids from around here go. Then I came back here with Griffin — that's my ex-husband. His family moved to New Bethlehem when he was about nine, but he considers himself a native anyway. And then I started practicing here. I guess I'd never thought much about living anywhere else."

"Any regrets?" Ruth immediately regretted asking such a personal question.

Belinda tilted her head to one side, and Ruth saw a flicker of sadness in her eyes. Her lips parted briefly, but she turned to place a serving bowl on the top shelf. "No, not really. Not about my career choices, anyway."

About what, then, Ruth wondered.

Lula stuck her head in the door. "Hi, honey, didn't want you to think we were ignoring you in here."

"Well, hey, Lula, glad you came over." Belinda's pensive expression broke into a smile.

Lula didn't look as glad. "Naomi's still kind of tired out, so maybe we'll visit another time," she said, almost in a whisper.

Greta appeared behind her; she was tall enough to look over Lula's head. "Are we still on for Thursday night?"

"You bet," Belinda said.

"I just don't know," Lula said in the same hushed voice.

"That's not our Naomi."

"Oh, for heaven's sake, Lula." Greta lowered her own voice. "Are you the same person you were ten years ago? Give the girl a chance to rest. She'll be fine."

Ruth smiled, never having thought of Naomi as a girl.

"Maybe you all can have lunch one day this week," Belinda said. "But please, don't give up."

The grandfather clock in the hall struck eleven. Ruth, curled up on the living room sofa with a book under a brass reading lamp, glanced at the photos on the end table beside her and on the fireplace mantel. There were plenty of Sarah, but most were of Eliza — classic cute-kid candids, a high school graduation portrait, a solemn wedding picture. One or two snapshots included Belinda and a redheaded, smiling man who must have been her husband at the time. In almost every snapshot, Belinda was doing something — lighting birthday candles, carving a turkey, holding a tiny Eliza's hand as they waded into a lake. Ruth recognized many of the faces in the larger family-gathering shots and black-and-white portraits from the photos she had carefully packed in Naomi's apartment on Estancia Boulevard.

She unfolded her legs and went to the mantel for a closer look at a picture of three little girls who looked suspiciously like Marina, Cara, and Eliza perched on a wooden fence, their hair blowing in the wind. Marina's grin was missing a couple of teeth, but she looked as if nothing could stop her from doing exactly what she wanted to do.

"Shit," Ruth muttered, turning away. How dense could she be to think that this trip would help her forget Marina? This was the family Marina had tried so hard to please, to protect from knowledge they couldn't handle. All of them had, in a way, sent her packing.

"See anyone you know in that lineup?"

Ruth jumped. "I didn't know you were there." Her cheeks grew hot.

Belinda leaned against the doorframe. "Didn't mean to sneak up on you. I didn't think anyone else was still up."

"Maybe my body's still on California time," Ruth said with a smile.

"I've heard of jetlag, but not carlag." Belinda laughed.

"I think I'll go to bed now, anyway." Ruth moved toward the stairs. She was in no mood for a photo show-and-tell of Marina at every adorable juncture in her life.

"Good night," Belinda said, looking after her.

Ruth lay in bed listening to the quiet, which was interrupted only by the occasional passing car. Naomi had every right to grieve, but did she have to sulk? Ruth's mother had taught her to always approach the world with either a smile or a composed frown; it was a surefire strategy for her lawyer mother in and out of court. Her father often escaped into his study for hours at a time, but he hardly ever moped. Everyone else had to shake it off and keep marching; why shouldn't Naomi?

Ed, Cara, Evan, and Marina had each carried away a piece of Naomi, and Ruth had escorted the remaining shell back to Indiana. Brilliant move. Naomi didn't want her around any more than Marina had.

She turned over, scrunched up the pillow, and remembered: *God is like a woman who won't rest until she finds what she wants.* It was the last thing she had ever expected to hear in church.

She had been a Sunday school regular at her parents' tall-steeple church, which stood at the top of twenty-four wide, gleaming white steps. At her confirmation, when she was fifteen, everyone stood in the light that shone through the stained-glass windows and promised to support and encourage her on her journey. Pinned to her dress was a red carnation which got crushed in several hugs after the service.

NANCY CROWE

Fueled by this newfound faith and affirmation, she found the courage not long afterward to tell her parents she was gay. There were no tearful confrontations, no forced visits to a therapist, no threats of exile. Her mother had defended many gay clients; people who had never met her associated the name Patricia Greene with justice for the cast-off and stepped-upon. Her father taught at a university where gay students, faculty, and staff were part of the academic and social landscape. Still, neither Patty nor Steve knew what to say to their daughter except that she would face harsh treatment in a world where prejudice begat prejudice, and every swing forward could be followed by a stinging backlash in the name of God or another deity of choice. And they loved her.

Ruth told only one other person, her best friend from youth group. On the group's next campout, the girls in Ruth's tent — who had been briefed by her confidante — kicked her out and she spent the cold, cloudy night under a tree in an on-and-off drizzle. That didn't stop one of the girls from telling everyone that Ruth had made a pass at her in the tent after the others were asleep. When Ruth and her parents met with the senior pastor, he suggested they find somewhere else to worship. They never returned to that church or any other.

During Ruth's sophomore year in college, Tina, who worked in the university bursar's office, invited her to a campus Christian fellowship meeting. "It's very open, not preachy at all. Really," she'd said. Ruth learned a few things in Bible study. She learned a few other things from Tina, a self-described former lesbian who had a picture of the crucified Christ with the words, *His Pain — Your Gain* over her bed.

By the time Ruth met Marina, she was ensconced in San Francisco's lesbian social and political scene, her identity no longer an issue for her or anyone else. She wrote grants to support lesbians in the arts and circulated petitions against anti-gay discrimination, domestic or abroad. And she had resolved never again to have anything to do with organized religion.

Ruth got up to open the window a little wider; it was a cool night and she needed some air. Maybe there were a few isolated places on the planet where you could sing, in a room full of people, about God's love and know that there would be no qualifiers or conditions tacked on down the line, but she doubted it.

Chapter Five

Naomi sat up in bed and rubbed her eyes and neck, trying to stuff the thoughts back in. She shuffled into the bathroom and avoided the mirror. It would reflect the same old face with the lines a little deeper, the mouth a little harder, and the hair making her look like a dandelion gone to seed. Marina would always tell her when it was time to go to the beauty parlor. Now no one cared how she looked or cared about seeing her at all, and she didn't care either.

She pulled on some clothes, dug through the debris in her suitcase for her tennis shoes, and went downstairs. No one else was up, and no paper was on the front porch or the driveway. Belinda must only take it on Sundays. There used to be a newspaper box in front of the drugstore, which might have been within walking distance twenty years ago, maybe even ten. She reached for the car keys.

Back home agaa-aain, in Indiaaaa-naaaa. The song had drifted through Naomi's mind as they crossed the state line Saturday. She couldn't remember the rest.

She drove down Belinda's street of brick and limestone houses with wrought-iron gates, watching the morning walkers hurry along the sidewalk in shorts and sweats and recognizing none of them. For the thousandth time, she wondered if she should go to a hotel rather than impose on her cousin. Especially with Ruth along. There was the Roadway Inn just east of town, if it hadn't been condemned or torn down. For all she'd known two days ago, barreling down the highway toward home, there could be a big chain hotel downtown now, the kind where you had Mother's Day brunch in a dining room with lots of fake plants and sneaked the kids into the indoor pool.

There wasn't, but the town square looked like a painting someone had added details to years after it was finished. Maybe the streetlights had been replaced, or a building had been torn down or repainted. Down by the courthouse, an old man in a stained gray jumpsuit swept the sidewalk and two women in jeans and green T-shirts pulled weeds from the big diamond-shaped flower beds on the corner. The stately limestone bank where Naomi's father had taken what money he earned still stood at Second and Main. God knew how many different banks it had housed since then. Schnierman and Sons, the little department store where her mother had taken her and her brother and sisters to buy new clothes when the family could afford them, had been turned into offices. She wondered if it still smelled like freshly roasted peanuts just inside the door.

Naomi drove slowly down Second Street. They'd passed a motor inn on the way into town, she recalled fuzzily. It looked halfway decent, but what had been in that spot before? Even a motor inn would be awfully expensive. Better to save the money and fly Ruth back to San Francisco as soon as the girl had sense enough to go. Surely she'd get bored in New Bethlehem and realize there was absolutely no reason for her to be here.

That last day on the road felt like they'd driven all the way to Maine, realized they missed an exit somewhere, and had to turn back. Naomi had been in a hurry to leave the motel that morning and Ruth had obliged, whisking their bags out to the car just as the sun came up. She'd put on one of her women's lib T-shirts and hadn't taken much time with her hair. She looked like one of those unkempt radicals, and that's what Naomi knew she would be bringing to Belinda's door. Ruth had hardly opened her mouth the whole day, except to yawn. Naomi knew she hadn't been sleeping much.

"Do you need the atlas?" Ruth had asked after they got off the interstate and onto a two-lane state highway. She'd reached for it under her seat.

"No!" Naomi met Ruth's startled gaze and regretted her tone. "I don't think Indiana's changed much in ten years."

"Well, let me know if it looks like somebody moved a road since you left, and I'll navigate." A hint of a smile had curved her lips.

Marina had brought home a friend or two before, but none like this one.

The drugstore was right on the corner where she left it, although it bore the lime-green logo of a national chain and newspapers were sold inside instead of outside in a box. Damn paper cost fifty cents now. The world's lousy news wasn't worth that much, but she bought it anyway.

On the way out of the store, she nearly collided with a young mother carrying a baby in one of those slings like Cara used. The baby was about the same size as Evan, just a shade too big to fit comfortably in one arm, with the same big eyes and tufts of downy brown hair on his sweet little head. Naomi froze.

"Sorry." The young woman pulled the infant closer and edged out of Naomi's way. The baby looked over his mother's shoulder, watching Naomi until a display of shiny plastic pinwheels diverted his eye. He did not make a sound.

Naomi forced herself to walk out the door and get back into the car, tossing the overpriced paper onto the passenger's seat. Evan had hardly ever been that quiet in public, but she hadn't really noticed. She'd taken him to church and never cared how loudly he bawled.

She couldn't buy this sudden infant death crap the doctor had tried to feed them that night. She had stood stupidly under those goddamn glaring hospital lights with all manner of life and death flying by, trying to figure out why Cara had called Marina before she called her own mother, and now this idiot was trying to tell her that a perfect, healthy baby was gone. Babies didn't die like that. They just didn't, unless someone did something horribly wrong.

Cara and Oliver were not churchgoers. When they got engaged, they were going to have a nice wedding at Naomi's church, but Cara canceled everything at nearly the last minute and opted to go stand in front of some bald old judge they'd never even heard of. By that time, Naomi had reserved the sanctuary, picked out the music and lined up a singer, ordered the food and flowers, proofed and sent the invitations, and paid for most of it. All that work, all that money, and Cara decided it was too much. She wouldn't say another word about it. Well, she did call the night before the ceremony to tell her when they were going to meet in the judge's chambers.

Everyone at Naomi's church whispered over the wedding of the year that didn't happen. Despite this humiliation, Naomi made arrangements to have Evan's funeral at her church. The senior pastor was off on some mission trip, so she was forced to ask that nincompoop of an associate. If he screwed this up, she vowed she'd have his balls on a shish kebab.

Naomi put on the dress she only wore to funerals, a dark silk one with a floppy bow tie. They all sat in the sanctuary, which was so quiet you could hear the beams and roof creak and settle, and listened to him talk about the resurrection and the life. Sunshine blazed in through the stained glass picture of Jesus with his arms out to the little children, the ones he cared about. The tiny flower-covered casket stood front and center, just out of the afternoon light. It should have been her in that casket. It should have been her own funeral, not Evan's.

Cara's boss let her take some time off. Naomi drove down every day or two just as she had when Cara was pregnant and then when her grandson was alive and real. She fixed Irish stew and honey barbecued chicken with mashed potatoes, Cara's favorite foods, and brought her cups of tea in bed. Cara stared across the room at that empty crib where Evan's breath had left him, and Naomi held her and rocked her as if she were the baby. Someone did wrong, no doubt about it, and they'd damn well better find out what it was before Cara and Oliver tried again. Wasn't the nursery monitor working? When did she last check on him that night? Had she held him wrong? What did the doctor say at Evan's last checkup? Cara didn't want to talk about any of that. She cried, and Naomi tried to console her all over again, but she would not be comforted. She was like that Rachel in the Bible, weeping for her children because they were no more.

Once when Naomi and Cara were talking in the kitchen and Cara got teary again and raised her voice, Oliver came in and said it was time for Naomi to leave. He had never spoken to her that way before, and she decided not to give him a chance to do it again. She'd visit Cara only when he was at work, and it would be a good long time before she fixed that lasagna he liked so much.

Naomi told herself she still had her girls, and maybe the Lord had cut her an even bigger break than she thought by letting her have them. At her age, one or both of them could have come out Mongoloid, although they weren't called that anymore. They could have been stillborn, died in their cribs for no reason that anyone could see, or never been born at all. Instead, they'd walked and run through Naomi's life, one tall, dark-haired, and serious; the other petite, blonde, and full of sunshine. Though Cara was more like her mother, Naomi had always been closer to Marina. Maybe that's the way it was with firstborns.

Now, after the fourth or fifth deep breath, she started the car and backed out of the drugstore parking space. She'd had her will redone, she remembered, just after Evan was born, so she could make sure he got her old stamp collection and the army of toy soldiers. Her brother Arnold had saved to buy those soldiers, one by one, back in the thirties and forties and she didn't want the girls to box them up for a church rummage sale or sell them to some slimy antique dealer. Now she'd have to do the will all over again as if Evan never existed, and she'd cut the girls out while she was at it. Even if the lawyer could find the girls when she died, they didn't need anything from her.

The car felt light and quick without that blasted trailer. You didn't realize what you were dragging, and for how long, until suddenly it wasn't there. You could floor the gas pedal out of habit, still thinking you had it to pull along, and go flying forward before you knew what was happening.

Naomi Sweet, Lula had called her. It hadn't been her name for ages, but that was how Lula, Greta, and a few others in town first knew her. Now it was a wonder they recognized her. Greta had become even more of a beanpole than she was in her teens; the surgery she'd had a while back must have been hard on her. She still had that long hair she always put up no matter how pretty Naomi told her she would look with it down, and that almost birdlike way of looking around like she was interested in everything. Age had revised her, but even a passing glance would tell you that this was Greta. Time had been kinder to Lula; she looked much the same as when her boys were tearing up the hardwood over at the school, but people with money didn't age as quick. It was a known fact.

She had every intention of going back to Belinda's house — although probably no one missed her — but the car some-

NANCY CROWE

how took her around the corner and past the turnoff for Wiggins Driveshaft, which was rarely called anything but "the factory" even though just as many people worked at the corporate headquarters next door. It was an imposing building with bright white columns and had been designed by some famous architect; the higher-ups at Wiggins had always made sure their offices, and their town, made a good impression.

Decades ago, Ed had walked through those wooden double doors and stopped to look at the small fountain in the lobby, a cherub holding a pitcher of water. He'd just stood there like a little towheaded boy someone stretched out and dressed up. Then he adjusted his tie, set his face to look serious, and strode up to the desk to apply for a job. Naomi had been working in the front office for about a year since she finished high school, and she'd been getting behind; a pile of letters waited to be typed that day. Then this damn charmer had waltzed in with his sad story about the military turning him down on account of his heart murmur.

"It still works, though," he'd said, patting his chest. It was then that Naomi noticed his hands — as delicate as a woman's, and yet they looked capable of wrapping themselves around a tree trunk and pulling it down.

Over tenderloins at Richie's, he'd told her all about his plans — investments, mail-order businesses, and the like. Until then, the factory would do.

"What's your favorite sweet thing on the menu, Naomi?" he asked when they finished eating.

She looked up. Richie Sr. had often given her brother and sisters free scoops of ice cream, without a word, when Naomi brought them in. "Why, a hot fudge sundae, I suppose."

Ed waved to get the attention of the young man behind the counter. Irvin Robinson was working the soda fountain and he strolled over like he was doing them a huge favor.

"A hot fudge sundae for the young lady, if you please," Ed said, "and a chocolate soda for me."

Irvin raised one eyebrow. "But of course, sir," he said with a little bow, the curl on top of his head bobbing with him. Irvin had been back from the service for three months and would marry her best friend, Greta, in another three. He'd been damn lucky to come home in one piece, but war had not humbled him.

Ed reached across the table and took Naomi's left hand in both of his. They were smooth, not a callus on them. "Naomi, do you believe in taking what some people call leaps of faith?"

Naomi tried, but could not stop herself from blushing. "I don't know."

Irvin brought their order and stood there holding the tray like some English butler. "Bon appetit, madame and monsieur." He set down the sundae and soda, bowed again ever so slightly, and departed.

Ed picked up his glass and clinked it against hers. He looked down at the table, suddenly shy as a schoolboy. "I don't know either, but I think this sundae's my first investment."

He took her back to the factory, and she had some explaining to do after an hour-and-a-half lunch. She quit when they got married, figuring she'd be pregnant within months, if not weeks. If she'd known it would be pushing twenty years, she might have stayed.

She turned down Standish Street. The houses were little boxes lined up like Monopoly game pieces, or maybe they just looked that way compared with Belinda's street, one of the nicest in town. Belinda had grown up in that big old house with the tiny back yard; she'd never known anything else. Everyone else in the family had either farmed or worked at the factory, and some did both. But Belinda's father somehow ended up being the owner and president of a small but powerful investment firm. Naomi and Ed sometimes had dinner over there when Belinda was just a girl, in that dining room with its polished woodwork and paintings of Parisian street scenes.

NANCY CROWE

Belinda always excused herself to do her homework; even then she knew what she had to do and set right to it. Belinda had always been a pretty girl. Not prom queen pretty, but fresh and solid and real. You knew where you stood with Belinda, and you knew you'd do well to stand near her.

And every damn time they went over there, Ed had to bend Uncle Jemison's ear about an investment strategy or stock. Naomi always gazed across the table at the impeccably attired Aunt Violet and tugged at the hem of her own dress, wishing it were just a little bit newer, a little less obviously homemade or purchased at a secondhand store.

Naomi looked to her left. The Nelsons had let their place go. If they still lived there, if they still lived at all. The people next door to the Nelsons had painted their house lime green like a Chinese restaurant, maybe thinking it would blend in with the weeds that clung like scared kids around the house, driveway, and lamppost.

She brought the car to a stop by the curb. This was the house she and Ed had bought when they were first married, a ranch with white siding, black shutters, and a one-car garage they quickly filled with junk, even though junk was about all they had. Ed used to park his old Ford in the driveway; he'd start whistling as soon as he passed that first bush with the red berries on it. That's how Naomi knew he was home.

Later, Marina helped her plant roses along the side fence. She couldn't seem to handle the plants without getting pricked. After hearing Marina yelp for the third or fourth time, Naomi had pulled her eight-year-old daughter into her lap. They sat together on the lawn, listening to the birds practice their early-spring songs. "Sometimes you have to put on those big gloves like Daddy's got and just grab 'em," Naomi said.

Now the bushes and roses were gone, making the fence and the front of the house look almost indecently bare. The place obviously hadn't been painted since they'd sold it ten years ago, and it needed it then. Two pickup trucks, one with a broken rear window, sat in the driveway. On the front porch, barely visible past the overgrown hedges, were assorted garish plastic toys and an easy chair with a long rip in the upholstery. Naomi caught a glimpse of a big dog, one of the mean breeds, tied to the chain-link fence in the back yard. He looked at her but did not bother to bark.

Some folks just didn't care how they lived, and maybe they were the smart ones. She put the car in gear.

Chapter Six

The office of Belinda Boaz, M.D., sat between a second-hand clothing store and a pawnshop. The one-story building looked like a gingerbread house, with hosta lilies and petunias lining the walk from the street. A design of some kind of plant, maybe wheat or barley, was carved into the polished front door.

"Griff did that for me when I bought this place," Belinda said to Ruth, unlocking the door. "He learned woodworking as a Boy Scout, and he's kept up with it ever since."

The first thing Ruth noticed when they stepped inside was the aroma: Belinda's scent combined with antiseptic and potpourri. Slowly, she turned around; this was not like any doctor's office she had ever seen. The front door opened into what might be someone's parlor, if not for the receptionist's desk and computer. A half-dozen chairs, some of which matched, and a coffee table stood to one side.

Belinda gave her the grand tour. A room at the back of the house had been turned into a comfortable meeting space; it was dotted with plants, chairs, a couple of scratched-up end tables, and even a beanbag chair. Ruth hadn't seen a beanbag chair since her parents sold a couple of them at a garage sale when she was about ten.

One small, windowless room, which might have been a closet or pantry, housed file cabinets and supplies. The examination room was like any other, except for a few cartoon prints on the walls. "It distracts patients who might be nervous," Belinda said, "even though I've known most of them a long time."

Another room had makeshift bookcases full of books, medical journals, haphazardly stacked magazines, brochures, and a spiral notebook for patients to check materials out. "I decided I wasn't busy enough as a doctor, that I'd be a librarian, too," Belinda said with a smile. "Actually, it's pretty low-maintenance, and it does help educate. You'd be surprised at what people don't know."

A large desk strewn with papers was the centerpiece of Belinda's office. "Insurance," she grumbled. The walls were covered with diplomas and certificates, photos of Eliza and Sarah, more colorful prints, and artwork by Sarah and some of Belinda's young patients. In front of the window hung a mobile of delicate amethyst crystals dangling from a gold hoop.

"This is beautiful." Ruth reached up to touch one of the crystals. "Did someone you know make it?"

"Yes. She doesn't live here anymore, though," Belinda said. She looked through the papers on her desk.

Ruth raised an eyebrow. "She moved away?"

Belinda nodded. "To Detroit, a while back. She still makes jewelry, mobiles, dream catchers and the like, and sells them at festivals. Probably not out your way, though. She mostly sticks to the Midwest." She motioned Ruth toward the hall. "I better show you where everything is up front before the phone starts ringing."

Except for the kitchen and bathroom, the floors were covered with standard blue office carpet. "Someone at church got me a good deal on this." Belinda tapped it with the toe of her low-heeled leather pump. She gestured toward the wallpaper and draperies, which bore a vaguely Southwestern blue diamond pattern. "Eliza pretty much did the rest. When I bought this place, she and Mark were over here every spare evening and weekend with their dust mops and paint brushes."

Sunlight beamed through the bowed picture window in front. Belinda opened one of the side windows and turned to Ruth, who was looking at the tiny framed pictures the unknown Renee kept on the desk. Each photo featured the same chunky toddler with a befuddled grin. "Ruth, I have to tell you I'm impressed."

"With what?" Ruth had been about to tell her how impressed she was with the office.

"With your being here," Belinda said. "Naomi hasn't said very much. Before she called a couple of weeks ago, I hadn't heard from her in years, other than Christmas cards. I know she had to have been devastated when the baby died, and it sounded like Marina and Cara moved away rather suddenly."

Ruth nodded. "Cara didn't even say where in Texas she was going, and Marina... well, she left a post office box number. They both... said they didn't want to see or talk to her."

"God, how painful." Belinda sighed. "I had a feeling it was something like that, but I didn't think I should ask too many questions. Then she shows up here with you." She leaned against the file cabinet behind the front desk. Her voice lowered ever so slightly, even though they were alone in the building, and her eyes seemed to roam the room before meeting Ruth's. "How long were you and Marina together?"

Ruth knew Belinda had weighed those words very carefully. "About two years," she replied. She studied the unevenly woven throw rug on the floor. "How — did Naomi tell you..."

Belinda's expression relaxed. "Heavens, no. I'm relying purely on intuition, and feel free to tell me it's none of my business. She knows, then?"

"Yeah." Ruth shrugged. "Marina never told her, but she

knows."

Belinda ran her hand along a shelf. "They say mothers always do. If my mother were still around, I'm sure she'd figure it out about me... maybe she already had. She was one smart lady. Never graduated from high school, but boy, she could size people up in a heartbeat. And the operative word there is heart." She picked up a round glass paperweight and shifted it from hand to hand. "The last time I saw Naomi, I was still married. So I don't think she's guessed."

"No, probably not." Ruth's smile faded. "I don't think she's picking up on other people's vibes right now, anyway."

"I know." Belinda sighed. She put down the paperweight and bent to adjust a stack of magazines on an end table, which was covered with an old-fashioned lace runner. "So Marina left, and you drove all the way out here with her mother. That's what I'm impressed with." She glanced up at Ruth again, her face a shade or two pinker than it had been a moment ago.

Ruth looked away. "I don't think I've done her any good. She's hardly said a word since we left San Francisco... since Nevada, anyway. That's about as unlike Naomi as anything I've ever seen."

"You're not kidding. Mom used to call her a babbling brook, among other things." Belinda shook her head. "Seriously, Ruth, you've done something very special, and it hasn't gone unnoticed. Yesterday she said something about you getting her out here in one piece, more or less."

Ruth stared at her. "Naomi said that?"

"Not very loud, but she did." Belinda smiled, a little sadly. "And it sounds like you've been through some rough stuff yourself."

Ruth exhaled slowly. "Marina would never acknowledge our relationship... even to herself, it seemed at times. For almost the whole time we were together, Naomi kept trying to set Marina up with someone's son or nephew. Sometimes

Marina begged off, but other times she'd meet the guy just to keep Naomi quiet. Then she'd tell her mom that he just wasn't her type or that he seemed too busy with his career. And she and I usually got into a fight when she went on these blind dates."

"*Blind* is right." Belinda's eyes were far away. Slowly, they focused on Ruth again. "That wasn't fair to anyone."

"No, it wasn't." Ruth realized she was pouring out her breakup story to someone she had met only two days ago, someone related to one of the principal players — two, counting Naomi. But there was no turning back now. "Things got a little better after Cara had her baby. But when the baby died, and then especially after Cara left... I guess Naomi got desperate. She told Marina the women's group at Naomi's church wanted to do a fundraiser for domestic violence victims and asked if Marina would come and talk to them about her work at the shelter. Well, Marina was pretty excited since this church has a lot of money and the shelter's been struggling to stay open. She made notes about what she wanted to say, and the shelter director gave her a box of brochures to take. So Naomi picked Marina up after dinner to go to the meeting."

"And?" Belinda had been listening intently, her eyes wide with a doctor's concern and a friend's shared dread.

Ruth swallowed hard and cleared her throat. "There was no meeting. Naomi took Marina to a restaurant for dessert and coffee with some guy she met in her dermatologist's waiting room and thought was a sure thing. Marina walked out. Naomi followed her and apparently they had a huge scene in the parking lot. Marina caught a cab home, came storming in the door and swore she'd never speak to her mother again."

"Good God." Belinda shook her head. "That's a hell of a stunt to pull, even for Naomi. What happened then?"

Ruth took a deep breath. "I asked if she didn't think it was time to end these games once and for all — with her mother and me and the rest of the world. She blew up and said she was tired of me trying to make her into someone she wasn't, and she wanted nothing more to do with me. Within a month, she'd lined up a new job in Seattle, packed her things, and left." Tears welled in Ruth's eyes; she blinked them back.

Belinda hesitated, moved a step closer, and put her arms around Ruth. Carefully, as if she thought Ruth might back away.

Ruth leaned into her. "I feel like such a coward." She breathed in Belinda's scent and felt her heart beating, and a tear escaped.

"Huh?" Belinda let go and looked her in the eyes. "Driving with Naomi from San Francisco, your home, to a place that must seem like another country and where you didn't know anyone — that sure doesn't sound cowardly to me. Especially after what you went through." She squeezed Ruth's shoulders.

Another tear pooled and Ruth had to look away, but not for long.

Belinda reached up as if to touch Ruth's hair, but gently patted her shoulder instead. "What can I say? God bless." She smiled, and then paused as if waiting for direction.

Ruth wondered what questions were formulating behind those blue eyes. The creak of the front door, loud enough that no bell was needed to announce someone's entry, startled her out of her musings.

Belinda moved toward the door to greet the elderly man. "Good morning, Lars. Have a seat and I'll be right with you."

"No hurry, Belinda," he replied with a smile. "I'm retired, remember?"

Belinda went to wash up. Ruth brushed at her eyes before she turned around to face the day's first patient. Her temporary medical gig in the middle of nowhere had begun.

The phone on the receptionist's desk required little explanation; all one had to do was push a clear button to send a call to Belinda's office or the exam room, or a red button to put a caller on hold. There was a button for the intercom, but Belinda said the office was too small to need it. A long-neglected stack of bills and records waited to be slipped into the proper manila folders in gray file cabinets, and Ruth began working her way through them.

"Don't worry too much about scheduling." Belinda had said earlier, putting her hands in her pockets. "If Charlene's not here, I can do lab tests and that sort of thing myself. Sure it takes extra time, but that's what's fun about a small practice."

Ruth stuffed a folder full of records back into the top drawer and slid it shut. It probably took a lot longer to come out in a small Indiana town; even in San Francisco, the process was rife with hills, dips, and curves in the road.

"How's it going?" Belinda's voice from somewhere in the office broke into her reverie.

Ruth nearly dropped another overstuffed folder. "No problem."

She wondered if Belinda was out to anyone else in town, and guessed the number of those in the know had to be pretty small. Being a woman doctor of the conventional orientation would be hard enough in a place like this.

While Belinda was with a patient and no one else waited, Ruth slipped into the library for a closer look. There were books on parenting, navigating the health care system, coping with arthritis, and quite a few on women's health. She pulled one off the shelf and looked through it; a chapter was devoted to lesbian health. It was just enough for any lesbian who happened to wander in and look around to guess that this might be a safe space. Relatively safe, given the surroundings. She turned toward the shelf nearest the window to find a row of books on mental health and the mind-body connection.

She was relieved not to see any titles on overcoming, healing from, repenting of, or otherwise rejecting homosexuality. Even in the office of a lesbian doctor, and a wonderfully kind and gentle one at that, the presence of such literature in a place like New Bethlehem would not surprise her. She had pored over one or two such books with Tina in San Francisco, capital of the civilized gay world, before the words and ideas congealed, hardened, and literally struck her.

The phone rang, and she dashed back to her temporary work station to answer it.

☙

Belinda introduced her to every patient who came in: a thirty-something grade school teacher off for the summer with two little kids in tow; an attorney in a snappy beige suit the same color as her carefully combed hair; a widowed grandmother who described each of her ailments to Ruth and found it all absolutely hilarious; a retired banker who wore a bright yellow bow tie.

She matter-of-factly made time to look at a red-faced child's aching ear and examine a very pregnant, very anxious girl who couldn't have been more than fifteen or sixteen. The young mother-to-be had been sick all weekend and wondered if something was wrong with the baby. Belinda put an arm around the girl's shoulders as she led her back to the exam room, telling her how rotten she had felt when she was pregnant with Eliza.

Others who dropped in just seemed to want to chat with Belinda. If she wasn't on the phone or with a patient, she took the person back to her office or simply sat down in the waiting area as if it were her living room. This amazed Ruth, who had never been to a doctor's office that wasn't overbooked and running at least half an hour behind, with people watching steel-knobbed doors and wishing they had stayed home. From her vantage point between inner office and outer office, she watched Belinda greet, question, listen, and reassure.

Charlene arrived promptly at ten. A dark-haired, stout woman somewhere between Ruth and Belinda in age, she wore the traditional nurse's white slacks and shoes with a royal blue blouse. There was an almost formidable Midwestern air about her, as if she might just as competently butcher your chickens and inoculate your hundred squealing piglets as take your blood pressure or bandage your wounds.

She nodded as she shook Ruth's hand. "It'll be good to have someone answering the phone out here," she said, moving briskly past Ruth to begin her day's work.

For the next few hours, Ruth watched her interact with patients and with Belinda. Charlene kept her eyes slightly downcast, saying only what needed to be said in a crisp, clear voice. With the children she spoke a little more softly, asking a little boy to tell her about his new bicycle as she deftly removed a splinter from his thumb.

Later in the afternoon, after Charlene had gone home, the stream of patients ran dry and the office settled into a rumpled stillness. Belinda said Ruth was free to go, that she'd done enough for one day, but Ruth opted instead to walk to Iaria's Pizza and Subs for a couple of sandwiches to go. The two jovial, dark-haired brothers who ran the place had already heard there was a new person working in Dr. Boaz's office, and she didn't get out of there without telling them where she was from and how she'd happened to come to New Bethlehem. They sent her back to the office with a complimentary order of breadsticks. She and Belinda ate in the waiting room, interrupted only a couple of times by the phone, and then went back to work.

"I forgot to tell you about our book group," Belinda called. Ruth followed Belinda's voice to the examination room, where the doctor was dusting the desk. "What kind of book group?"

"I guess that depends on when you ask. Or who. We meet one Thursday a month in that back room there, somebody brings dessert, and we discuss a book. Lula and Greta usually come, and Charlene. We didn't plan it to be all women, but that's how it's ended up. Anyway, you're welcome to join us. If you're still here on Thursday." Belinda looked at Ruth with the same questioning gaze she had earlier.

Ruth felt her neck grow hot. "That sounds great. I... guess I'll be here."

Belinda smiled. "I'm glad."

Ruth watched her run the cloth along each shelf above the counter. "Are you out to anyone here?"

Her eyebrows went up, and Ruth was afraid she had said the wrong thing.

Belinda shook her head. "A few people may have guessed, but..."

"Is there any kind of community around here?" Ruth asked.

Belinda shrugged. "Not that you'd ever notice. There's the guy who runs the bookstore around the corner, but I hardly know him. That's it as far as I know."

Ruth could not imagine such isolation. "That must be hard for you."

Belinda smoothed the paper on the examination table. The stirrups were covered with what looked like small, hand-knitted stocking caps which bore the name of a pharmaceutical company. No male doctor or marketing director would have thought of that.

"I guess the worst of it was when Annelise left... she's the one who made that mobile you were admiring earlier," Belinda said. "Since nobody knew about us, nobody thought twice about it when she moved away. It wasn't like when I got divorced. In a small town like this, you may or may not get a lot of support when you're going through a divorce; it all depends on who's talking to who and who believes which story. But at least everyone knows why you're not quite yourself."

Ruth had never thought about that.

"Well." Belinda tossed the dust cloth into a hamper under the counter. "Enough of my rambling. Back to the insurance forms." She put on her glasses and retreated to her office.

All remained quiet until Eliza virtually burst through the door wearing a red and white striped summer dress with white eyelet lace about the collar and sleeves. Ruth imagined Eliza had a house full of lace curtains. "Hey, Ruth. How'd your first day with Mom go?"

"Great." Ruth turned from the computer. "She's very easy to work with."

Belinda emerged from her office. "Hi, sweetie. You just get off?"

Ruth had learned the day before that Eliza worked in the accounting department at Wiggins, where Mark worked second shift in the warehouse.

"Yeah. I've got to pick up Sarah from 4-H, and then there's a Worship Committee meeting I completely spaced. Mark just called to remind me. Are you heading home pretty soon?"

Belinda looked at the clock. "No, I've got a few more insurance puzzles to figure out, and Elaine Sweeney's coming by for her allergy shot. Why don't you drop Sarah off at the house anyway? Naomi's there."

"Oh, I'd hate to impose." Eliza glanced at Ruth.

How could she look so fresh, Ruth wondered, after a day crunching numbers in a driveshaft factory? Whatever a driveshaft was.

Ruth hesitated, then offered, "I don't think she'd mind." If she noticed at all.

"They seemed to get along pretty well yesterday." Belinda fiddled with a pen; Ruth already knew that meant she was thinking. "Tell Naomi to call here if there's a problem. And pick up some chicken or something so she doesn't have to mess with cooking."

Like she'd done anything in a kitchen lately but mope. Naomi and Marina used to whip up huge feasts, making a disaster area of her kitchen or theirs, but usually producing something tasty or at least edible. By themselves, Ruth and Marina had tried a new recipe just about every week. No matter how the dish turned out, even if it was a total loss and they ended up eating cereal, they had always dined by candle-light.

"Ruth, is that okay?"

"I'm sorry, Eliza. What did you say?"

"I'll run back here and get you if Naomi's out or sleeping or something. If Mom can spare you, that is."

"Sure, that's fine," she agreed, hoping it wouldn't be necessary.

"I guess I can handle this mob on my own." Grinning, Belinda waved her hand toward the empty waiting area. "But I think Naomi and Sarah will do just fine. Pick her up in the morning, if you want."

Eliza hurried out again, the heels of her red ankle-strap shoes clicking on the entryway's hardwood floor. "Thanks, you guys."

"Those two." Belinda chuckled. "Mark and Eliza get their signals crossed so often it's a wonder they even had Sarah."

Ruth leaned on her elbows. "Is it rough on her, with them working at different times?"

"Sometimes, especially during the summer. But she just goes with the flow and seems to be turning out fine in spite of all of us."

"She's lucky to have you," Ruth said quietly.

No lights, not even the blue flicker of a TV screen, were on downstairs when they returned to Belinda's house.

"If that car wasn't here, I'd say Naomi and Sarah went out

for a night on the town." Belinda turned off the engine and reached for her briefcase.

"Is a night on the town possible here?" Ruth replied without thinking. "I mean, it seems pretty... quiet."

Belinda smiled and shut the car door. "Depends on your tastes."

Ruth went upstairs and paused at the door to what looked like Sarah's room-away-from-home. There they were, sitting on the floor amidst a sea of impossibly leggy Barbie dolls and associated paraphernalia, Naomi in her black gabardine slacks, a pale blue blouse with a ruffled neck, and her usual slippers. Her hair looked as if she'd at least taken a few obligatory swipes at it with a comb, and now she was busy braiding a doll's platinum locks. Apparently they hadn't heard Belinda and Ruth come in.

"Where's Barbie going tonight?" Naomi asked.

"On a trip." Sarah pulled a dress over her doll's head and threaded spiky plastic arms through tiny lace sleeves.

"Well, where's Ken?"

"Ken who?"

"You know, Barbie's boyfriend. Husband. Whatever." Naomi leaned over and pawed through a bright pink vinyl case. "Got to be a Ken in here somewhere."

"No. She's going with Heather." Sarah held up a doll with shiny brown hair.

"Oh."

Ruth stood perfectly still; if she so much as creaked a floorboard or breathed too loudly, she'd startle Naomi into the next county.

"Okay, what do these gals need for their trip?" Naomi rearranged her legs, grimacing a little.

"Nothin'. They're just going to California, and they're coming right back." Sarah had it all figured out.

"California, huh? That's a heck of a trip."

Ruth knew she couldn't stand there much longer. "Hi,"

she said just above a whisper.

Naomi jumped only slightly. "Well, hi. When did you get home?" Her native twang was more pronounced after only a couple of days back home, and despite being alone for most of that time. She twisted around to look at the clock on the night table. "Oh-oh, kiddo. Looks like bedtime for you," she told Sarah, who wrinkled her nose but did not protest. "Go on and say goodnight to your grandma. You got a toothbrush?"

"Yeah, I stay here all the time." Sarah thundered down the stairs.

Ruth looked at Naomi, sitting on the floor surrounded by Barbie dolls, some of them naked, and couldn't help chuckling.

"Don't just stand there. Help me up off this floor." She lifted her arms.

Ruth pulled Naomi to her feet, glad to see color in her cheeks. "Belinda has a great office. You should see it."

Naomi followed Ruth into the catch-all room. "I stay out of doctor's offices as much as I can, which isn't easy anymore. What'd you do all day?"

"I filed records and answered the phone. I haven't quite figured out the computer." She plopped down on the bed across from Naomi, who had settled into the desk chair. "I haven't operated any machine that keeps track of money since high school, and this looks pretty different from the cash register at the McTavish Inn."

Naomi snorted. "Kid, you should see the cash registers I worked in high school. They're probably sitting in a museum or antique shop somewhere."

"Were they the kind that had a crank on the side, went 'ding' when you rang up the sale, and shot the drawer into your stomach?"

"That's about it." Naomi examined her nails. "I was awful glad to get my job in the office at Wiggins. I could handle the typewriter and adding machine."

Ruth sat on the bed and tucked her legs under her. "I'll bet the town was pretty different then."

"A lot's been knocked down and put up." Naomi concentrated on her cuticles. "But you could always count on someone being there to give you a break, someone like Belinda. She's the smart one in the family, always knows what to do. I guess she's in the right line of work."

Ruth smiled. "I guess so."

"Around here you don't have to wonder where you belong or what you're supposed to do, or if something awful's going to happen to you or your kids if one of you talks to the wrong person. In San Francisco, unless you're a minority or a freak, you're out there on your own."

Ruth quietly let out the breath she had held. There was so much that she had never asked Naomi, and not just because Naomi had rarely given her the chance. She pulled up one leg and rested her chin on her knee. "Is there anything about San Francisco you like?"

"The winters were a hell of a lot better, I'll give 'em that." Naomi sighed. "You going back soon?"

Ruth's eyes wandered from the sailboat painting over the desk to the boxes in the corner and her suitcase on the floor. "As long as I'm here, I might as well help Belinda at the office, since her assistant's off. What are your plans?"

"Honey, at my age you don't plan. You just get by." She lowered her eyes. "That little girl could use some looking after."

"You two seemed to be having fun."

"She's a smart one, I'll tell you. Just like Belinda at that age," Naomi said. Her hands trembled, and she dropped them into her lap. "It's good you're helping her out."

Ruth laced her fingers together. "It's... I don't know. She introduced me to everyone who came in today, and I felt like I wasn't a stranger."

"Well, bless Belinda."

Ruth grinned. "Amen."

Naomi narrowed her eyes. "Just remember you're not in San Francisco anymore."

The Threshing Floor

Chapter Seven

Cover the World, the bookstore Belinda had mentioned, had the nicest storefront on the block — a fresh coat of cappuccino-colored paint with light yellow trim, window boxes full of red and blue impatiens, and a finely lettered sign. If Ruth had been walking down the street and had to guess which business was owned by a gay man, this would be it.

The inside was another story. Used books crowded ceiling-high shelves and wire display racks; some were stacked or sitting in open boxes on the floor. A cloth and bottle of glass cleaner had been left on top of a stack of books by the window. Ruth breathed in the scent of old paper, age-softened cardboard, and the accompanying dust. She and Marina had discovered a bookstore just like this on a rainy Saturday only weeks before Marina's departure. They'd forgotten all about their mission — to find new blinds for their patio door — and spent an hour or so browsing.

She was jarred back to the present as something metal and what sounded like several heavy books hit the floor in the back room, followed by several rumbling invectives. The door swung open and a tall man in his late thirties emerged, brushing dust from his blue shirt and wrinkled khakis. "I apologize for my language. I had a stack of books up to my chin when I heard the door, and when I went to set it down they all toppled and took the clipboard with them." He adjusted the cuffs of his sleeves and took a good look at Ruth. "I know who you are. You're from San Francisco and you're working for Dr. Boaz."

Ruth smiled. "I've only been here a couple of days."

He grinned behind a straw-colored beard. "I knew that, too."

"Do you know my name?"

"Afraid you've got me there. You'd have to be here a hell of a lot longer than a couple of days before I'd remember your name. But what the heck — I'm Will Polanski."

She shook his hand. "I'm Ruth Greene." Not that the name of a mere stranger in town would matter to him.

"So what in the world brings you to our little burg?" He folded his arms and leaned against the counter.

"I drove out here with a friend to help her get settled. She's from here and decided to move back."

"And that friend would be?" he asked impatiently.

"Naomi Bittner."

"Bittner, Bittner. Nope, doesn't ring a bell." He turned away from her. "Hi, what can I help you with?" He went to wait on a heavy, middle-aged woman who had just come in with two restless children in tow.

Ruth browsed the extensive Current Events and Politics area while Will showed the woman everything he had on fly fishing, providing a detailed explanation of what was in each, who wrote it, whether it or the author had any merit, and which of them her husband — who apparently went fishing with Will and some other men on a regular basis — might like the best. Almost twenty minutes later she bought three of them, pried her grandchildren out of the children's section, and left. By that time, a young man with fraternity letters on his T-shirt had come in and was scouring the shelves in the Literature section. Will greeted him like an old friend and helped him find two Shakespeare plays and *A Tale of Two Cities*. They spent several minutes talking about campus life, including the frat party Will and some friends had crashed in their college days, and the merits of various courses. Will, it seemed, had taken them all but never earned a degree due to his advisor's treachery and other misfortunes.

After the student left, Ruth strolled back toward the cash register. "So, have you lived here all your life?"

"Me? No, I moved here from Dayton with Al — God, it's going on eighteen years now. Then the sonofagun decided to get married and move to Iowa, of all places." He shook his head, picked up the dust cloth, and dabbed at the glass panes on the door. "Those rug rats get fingerprints all over my door every time Winnie brings them in here, bless her heart. Anyway, I was making good money at the factory, so I stuck around until I had enough to open this place. Oh, the hassles I had that year. Frank just about had to put me back together, piece by piece, after Uncle Sam and everyone else got through with me. If Frank hadn't had a good job, we'd have been in a padded cell or out on that corner with our little tin cups."

Will continued polishing the door, then tossed the rag over another display and began sorting through one of the boxes on the floor. All the while, he held forth on some tax law the governor had helped bring into being, how and why it would shoot small businesses down in flames, and how two other states had handled the same issues far more sensibly.

Ruth tried to discreetly look at her watch. Belinda had told her to take a good long lunch break because they'd be busy later, but this was pushing the boundaries of both good business behavior and Ruth's patience. She edged toward the door, but there was no exit from the conversation in sight.

"I have to get back," she said when Will paused to take a breath. "It was nice to meet you." She pulled the door open.

"Well, have a good one. Hey!"

Ruth turned around. She was never going to get out of this place.

"I hear you're a college professor."

"Actually, I'm an instr —"

"Come by again and we'll discuss the sorry state of education in this great country of ours. You really ought —"

"I'll do that." She was out the door. How could Belinda live in a town where the only other known — and "known" might be a relative term — gay person was a dust-covered windbag who couldn't be bothered with a visitor's name?

Naomi was right. She wasn't in San Francisco anymore.

"Well, I just don't believe it." Lula slammed her copy of *Fried Green Tomatoes at the Whistle Stop Café* onto the rickety end table beside her chair.

Ruth reached up to steady the wobbling table before the barely-brewed tea in Lula's cup could spill over. As the youngest of the women gathered in the informal meeting room in Belinda's office, Ruth had been assigned the beanbag chair. A cobweb-like silence settled over the book group.

Lula's late husband had been president of Wiggins, and she presided over several church and civic activities. According to Belinda, Lula was a regular at the high school basketball games, where her two sons had been heroes years earlier. She cheered unabashedly, as if the boys had never left the court, and was known to hurl scathing remarks at the referees.

"This is a perfectly nice story. I just don't believe the author would put a nasty thing like that in there." She smoothed her cotton skirt. She sat in a chair that might be called a wing-back; in any case, its back rose up taller than the others. Ruth could picture Lula at the end of a polished dining-room table, making pleasant small talk with her husband and reminding her sons to use their white linen napkins.

NANCY CROWE

"Well, it's not very… explicit, or anything like that," Greta said in her soft voice, eyes darting from Belinda to Charlene to Lula as if she regretted bringing up the possibility that two of the book's main female characters were more than friends.

"Then why did you say that, Greta?" Lula persisted.

Greta flipped through her book. She plucked some imaginary dirt from her jeans, which she wore cuffed with anklets and white tennis shoes. "I read in the paper that some people protested the movie because they didn't think it was explicit enough. If it was even there to begin with, which it may not have been at all." Her words tumbled over one another.

"Well, I saw the movie and read the book, and I certainly didn't think those two girls were… what you said." Lula shifted in her chair.

Belinda, the perennial hostess, had not said a word. She quietly paged through her book as if it were a medical reference tome, her lips in a straight line. Mindful of her presence on alien turf, Ruth kept her mouth shut.

"Those liberal perverts will protest anything," said Charlene, who had been quiet until now. "They want the rest of us to sanction their lifestyle. Some of 'em want to get married to each other, even. They allow that out in San Francisco?" She fixed her pale eyes on Ruth.

"Um, they… we have domestic partnership, and that's recognized by the City."

Charlene shook her head. "What a shame. I don't know how you stand it out there, all those queers."

Ruth's face flushed as crimson as the scarf she wore tied around her head. She looked at Belinda, who kept her eyes on the open book in her lap. This was her office, and she was being maligned. Why the hell didn't she say something?

"It's no secret that morality is declining everywhere you look," Lula said with a sniff. "The homosexuals get protection the rest of us don't. Even in a couple of places here in Indiana, they're pushing that. Why, if my husband had been forced by some law to hire one of them, you can bet there would have been trouble."

Ruth counted to ten and tried to ignore the fact that she was about two heads below Lula's eye level. "You don't believe that gays and lesbians have the right to work like everyone else?"

Lula turned toward Ruth. "Of course everyone has the right to earn a living, but no one should be forced to accept a lifestyle that goes against the laws of God and man."

"But it's not accepting a 'lifestyle,' whatever that means." Ruth's stomach knotted up. "It's just equal rights... under the laws of God and everybody else."

Lula drew back and dismissed Ruth with a wave of her hand.

Greta sat up straight. "Didn't West Jefferson pass a law not too long ago? It made a lot of people mad, but it got passed."

"In Indiana?" Ruth's eyebrows shot up before she could restrain them.

Greta nodded. "It barred discrimination against... gays. Just in employment, I think. I don't remember." Her gaze dropped back to her book.

"That's great," Ruth said. "We've had that for quite a while now."

"Maybe that's how they do things where you come from." Charlene leaned forward, both feet flat on the floor. "My husband and I moved here because he got a good job at the factory, but we stayed because this is a place where you can raise your kids right. There are still decent people in this world."

"There are decent people everywhere, Charlene," Greta said.

Belinda rose. "Would anyone like more coffee? There's plenty of decaf left, and I can put some more hot water on for tea." Hearing a couple of murmured affirmatives, she left the room.

86   NANCY CROWE

Ruth pulled at a loose thread on the beanbag, feeling very long-legged and close to the ground. She shouldn't have come; she should have known better than to expect anything but grief in the home town of the woman who had cast Ruth aside. Laws, lifestyle, perverts, God and man — it was the same damn string of words, just in a different order and from different mouths.

Charlene turned back toward Ruth. "Did that hurt?" She placed a finger on her own thin eyebrow.

"Yes, it did." Ruth gently touched the little gold ring. "But it healed." Many had stared, but few people in New Bethlehem had come out and asked her about her eyebrow ring.

"Well." Greta looked at her watch. "Why don't we talk about what we're going to read next?"

Ruth waited by the front desk for Belinda to finish the odds and ends she'd busied herself with after the book group adjourned. "Are you just about finished?" she called.

Belinda emerged from her office with a stack of files. "Ruth, I hope you weren't too put off by Lula and Charlene. They're both fairly good-hearted women with very big mouths."

"And very small minds." Ruth folded her arms. "How could you listen to that crap without saying anything? Especially Charlene. How can you work with someone with that kind of attitude?"

Belinda sighed. "I know there's no point in trying to change Lula's mind, or Charlene's mind, or any of the hundreds of other minds around here that think that way. Believe me, if I tried to defend gay rights in these circles, I'd alienate a lot of folks — not to mention the suspicions that would start to fly, and this little ol' practice doesn't need that." She brushed some dust off the computer monitor. "I know it must be hard for you to understand. It's different from what you're used to."

"I feel like I'm on another damn planet out here." Ruth began to pace.

Belinda watched her. "I always wanted to go to San Francisco."

Ruth whirled around. *Come back with me, then.* Her cheeks flushed for the second time that evening. "San Francisco has its problems, too." She tried to remember how to breathe. "Earthquakes and so forth."

"Here, it's tornadoes," Belinda said.

Ruth paced a few more steps. "You want to get a cup of coffee or something?"

"There's Richie's, down on Main." Belinda looked at the clock. "He's sometimes open late on weeknights. That's about it around here. No gourmet coffee shops."

"That's fine." She couldn't have cared less about gourmet coffee.

Richie's was the diner with the half-lit sign that Ruth and Naomi had passed when they arrived in New Bethlehem a few nights before. The inside was a shrine to the high school basketball team, with pennants and photos dating back several decades, and was decorated in the school colors, blue and yellow. Most of the blue and yellow vinyl seats bore at least one rip, cut, or cigarette burn, and a couple of them had been replaced or recovered in beige. Off to one side was an old jukebox, a gift from the class of '59.

Aside from two men hunched over their plates at the counter and a teenage straight couple huddled on one side of a booth, Belinda and Ruth had the place to themselves. They sat at one of the tables by the window.

"Evening, Belinda." A rotund man with glasses slipping down his nose and a mess of curly brown hair, wearing an apron that looked as if it hadn't been washed in weeks, plunked two glasses of ice water on their table. "What can I get you girls tonight?"

"Richie, I think we're just having coffee. Decaf for me,"

Belinda said.

"Me too." Ruth decided to let "girls" go; Belinda appeared not to have noticed. She probably got called a girl every day, even in her office.

He ambled behind the counter and reappeared with two cups of something that looked like motor oil. "I give those kids fifteen more minutes, and then I'm running 'em out of here," he told Belinda in a low voice, jerking his thumb toward the nuzzling couple. "This isn't exactly a romantic bistro, and I don't want the cops jumpin' down my throat because I let somebody stay in here past curfew."

"I guess you have to, the way they've been cracking down lately." Belinda stirred sweetener into the muddy brew.

Richie strolled back to the kitchen, clearing his throat and glancing at the clock on the wall as he passed the young lovebirds.

"We've had a problem here lately with kids being out at all hours and getting into trouble," Belinda explained. She stirred her coffee some more. "This isn't such a bad little town, you know."

Ruth nodded. "I didn't mean to suggest that it was. It's just different. I grew up in San Francisco, and whenever I've traveled very far it's been to someplace like New York. And I was always with my parents or friends who were from California too, even if they'd lived somewhere else before."

Belinda smiled. "Griff and I took Eliza to Texas on one of her school breaks, but that's as far west as I've ever been."

Ruth sipped her coffee; if it were not decaffeinated, they'd be up all night. "It sounds like the two of you are on pretty good terms. I mean, he carved that design on your door and all."

"Griff's a good man," Belinda said. "He went through what I guess you'd call a midlife crisis. There was no outlandish behavior, but he suddenly had no clue what he wanted from life. I guess I wasn't much help."

"God, that must have hurt," Ruth said.

Belinda nodded. "We still had to deal with each other because of Eliza, and we managed to be civil. Once some time passed, we kind of got to know each other as friends again. We both admitted there were things we could have handled better."

"Did you... did he know about your sexuality?"

"I've often wondered," Belinda said. "I didn't really know that about myself until after we were divorced." She turned the cup slowly around on its saucer. "Anyway, he was real supportive when I started my own practice. By that time, he'd moved to Indianapolis — his real estate company expanded. Still, he came here to pick up Eliza for weekends with him before she started driving. He built me a couple of bookshelves when the ones that came with the place gave out on me."

"That's wonderful," Ruth said. "I don't see any kind of post-breakup bond developing with Marina." She absently fingered a packet of artificial sweetener. Talking about Marina was no more painful than thinking about her, which Ruth had done plenty of — but saying her name still brought a heavy ache.

"No, not from what you've said. Annelise kept in touch for a while after she left town, but it's been a few years now since I've heard from her. Guess she's moved on, and that's fine."

Ruth studied Belinda's calm, reserved face. "Did you two break up before she moved?"

"I think we probably would have broken up even if she'd stayed," Belinda said. "We were both scared to death of losing our kids. She had two little boys and her ex-husband worked at the factory, where she did. And I just wasn't ready then for something permanent. Of course, it's easier to see that now," she added. "Annelise got the job offer in Detroit and said she wanted to get a fresh start. She pretty well left without a backward glance, like the relationship either wasn't much or didn't exist. And it didn't, as far as anyone else knew."

"What about Eliza?" Ruth asked. "Did she know?"

"Heavens, no. We were very careful about that." Belinda paused. "At least I don't think she did. She's always had this way of turning her head to one side and looking like she's listening to you, but you know she's thinking — God knows what." She shook her head. "Anyway, she was a teenager and had her own things to worry about."

"She seems to worry a lot now," Ruth said. "That's my impression, anyway."

Belinda chuckled. "Bless her heart, she's always been that way. She didn't want any of her friends to know when her dad and I split up... but word gets around in a place like this."

"I'll bet," Ruth said.

"Mark's been good for her," Belinda said. "She'll try to do ten things at once and have them all come out perfect, and he just shrugs his shoulders and adores her."

Ruth laughed. A love song played on the jukebox. "So, Eliza still doesn't know?"

Belinda sighed, and shook her head. She examined the inside of her coffee mug, tipping it toward her. "When I was with Annelise, and then when she left... at that point in my life, I figured that's just the way it was. You find love, and the price is having to keep it a secret. If it lasts."

The teenagers had left and the jukebox stopped, leaving the muffled voices of the men at the counter and Richie's occasional whistling in the background. Ruth glanced across the chipped table at Belinda and decided she could sit there with her all night. She could tell herself it was the coffee that caused her stomach to do gymnastic flips, but it would have been a lie.

A yellowed black-and-white photograph of what might be Belinda's church, but could be any church, hung slightly off-kilter on the wall near their table. "Yours must have been a churchgoing family for a long time," Ruth said. "Just about all of you seem to be pretty involved."

"My grandfather, Naomi's uncle, was a minister." Belinda sat back in the blue vinyl chair. "He was pastor of our church for years, and he put the fear of God in just about everyone who ever talked with him. A few older members can recall his Sunday scold-and-steam. That's what folks used to call his sermons."

"It sounds like some kind of dry cleaning process," Ruth said, chuckling. "How'd they get from him to Jim Foster in the same century?"

Belinda smiled. "Jim's one of a kind — no one's really sure what kind. Greta was on the search committee, and they didn't know quite what to make of him and some of his 'out-there' ideas. He spent years in the corporate world, and I guess they finally decided he was someone who had learned from real-life experiences and mistakes and not just from studying the Bible. I think they were ready for that. What about you?"

Ruth fingered the packets of sugar and sweetener in their cracked china holder. "I got tired of being alone on Sunday mornings... and I guess I wanted to share something that was so important to Marina. But I just couldn't join." She was quiet for a moment. "My family went to church too, until I started coming out."

"Oh, no." Belinda shook her head. "You'd think the churches out there would be a little more open. How old were you?"

"Fifteen."

"Fifteen?" Belinda leaned her chin on her hand. "I don't think I had a clue when I was twice that age. So you didn't go again until you met Marina?"

"Well, not exactly. In college I went to one of those campus Christian fellowship things right after a breakup. It was actually fun until I developed what I guess you'd call a particular friendship with one of the leaders. Tina was a so-called former lesbian who'd found the Lord, and she was a recovering alcoholic and drug addict. But one thing led to another, and… well, she just lost it. She claimed I'd dragged her down into sin, and started slapping me in the face and punching me in the stomach. Then she outed me to the rest of the group, and everyone very piously prayed for my deliverance, then literally locked me out of the room." Ruth looked searchingly at Belinda, who was listening wide-eyed.

Belinda rubbed her forehead. "I'm surprised you can come to church with me after all that."

"I guess I still have hope." She wanted to reach across the table for Belinda's hand, but she reached for a water glass instead and took three big gulps.

❧

Ruth and Belinda stood under a tree whose branches concealed them in a soft green canopy. It could have been the oak in Belinda's front yard or a California cedar, but it didn't matter where they were because Belinda's warmth wrapped around her as sunshine poured through the leaves. Slowly they sank to the ground and with a light, sure touch, Belinda stroked Ruth's hair and leaned forward to brush her lips against Ruth's…

Ruth sat up in bed, heart pounding. She looked around the room in the faint light between dark and dawn, at the desk, chair, teddy bear, dresser, boxes, and shadows of her own belongings.

She started as a floorboard creaked in the hall. Had Belinda heard Ruth's dream, sensed it from down the hall? A minute later, the toilet flushed. Nope, it had to be Naomi; the woman had a bladder the size of a garbanzo bean.

Ruth turned her pillow over to "change the channel" the way she had as a child, to get rid of whatever had invaded her consciousness. She had come to New Bethlehem to settle the unsettled and fill in the gaps. That was all. If she couldn't do that without starting down a road marked "Closed," she'd better get her butt back to San Francisco.

Chapter Eight

"See that house over there?"

Ruth shaded her eyes from the setting sun. "That one with the blue trim?"

"Yep." Naomi had decided it was time to start taking her evening walks again, something she'd always done in New Bethlehem: Hand in hand with Ed just before dark, then pushing the girls in strollers, and later trying to keep up with Marina on her fitness walks. In San Francisco you never knew what you might run into around the next corner, so she'd stopped. "That's where my high school sweetheart lived. Bobby Rinderknecht." She pronounced the name easily. Naomi Rinderknecht, she had mouthed over and over in front of the bathroom mirror fifty years ago.

They turned down another street lined with houses of about the same vintage as Belinda's house, some looking like they were tired of standing there taking up space. Others had been fixed up, probably by young couples who'd figured out the older places were built better.

"Were you going to marry him?" Ruth asked.

Ruth set her stroll to match Naomi's. How she managed to walk in those boots without clumping along like a Clydesdale, Naomi would never figure out. Wearing them with shorts made her look like some kind of mountain climber.

"He gave me his class ring and told me the next ring he gave me would have a diamond in it. When he had more money. His family was pretty well off, so I didn't know what was holding him up, but I believed him."

"So what happened?"

"He got a girl pregnant over in Waynesville." Naomi's voice had flattened.

Ruth slowed her steps and pushed her blonde-brown hair, which had grown down to her shoulders, behind her ear. She always did that when she wanted to see something better, or even hear something better. "Oh, Naomi."

Why did that sound so sad to Ruth? Half the children in San Francisco didn't know who their daddies were. "Now believe you me, that wasn't something that happened much back then, at least not around here. And it sure wasn't talked about. I haven't talked about it myself in years." Naomi said, patting her own hair into place. She'd splurged and gone to Yvonne, who still ran a beauty parlor out of her basement. She'd put the blonde and gray back into balance and added a little wave, which didn't wave much in an Indiana summer. She looked down the street, searching the front of each dwelling for a porch, gate, or door that would identify it with this friend or that relative. She had been doing that since she arrived from California — trying to match the pictures in her head with what was in front of her.

Ruth was quiet, but Naomi knew she was listening and thinking. "He married her real quick, and they lived with her folks at first," Naomi said. "They told everyone the baby was premature and that he and I'd been broke up a long time before he got with her. But you can only tell so many tales in this town."

"That stinks."

They resumed their pace, stepping over a cluster of faults

in the sidewalk. Neighbors sitting on their porches or pulling weeds in their front yards nodded or waved their hellos. Naomi thought she recognized one or two of them, but she wasn't sure enough to say anything. The teenagers driving by in their dusty hand-me-down sedans and station wagons could be the grandchildren of her classmates, but you never knew. More than one well-meaning stranger over the years had assumed that Marina and Cara were her granddaughters.

"Well," Naomi said, "young folks get over these things, and I met Ed not too much later."

"Did you ever talk with Bobby again?"

Naomi had stood halfway down the steps of the bank, watching Bobby hand the plump baby boy to his plump young wife, kiss her goodbye right there on the corner at lunch hour, and go whistling back down the street to his daddy's office. Everything Naomi had felt for him — maybe everything she had felt, period — rose and threatened to spill over, and she wasn't sure if she was going to cry or throw up.

"Oh, I saw him around town every now and then, usually with her and the baby. That was the cutest little baby you ever did see. Until mine came along, that is." She tugged at a curl near her ear. "I guess that was the hardest part. That baby of his came into the world by accident, and I couldn't get pregnant even after being married all those years. That kind of stuck in my craw." But it was nothing like being eliminated from the life of one child, then the other.

"Stuck in your what?" Ruth turned to look at her, one eyebrow raised.

Naomi cleared her throat and patted Ruth's shoulder. "It's an expression, honey."

Ruth laughed. "Does it have anything to do with crawfish?"

"Crawdads? I really don't know."

"I guess I need to learn the language around here," Ruth said.

"You probably get the important stuff," Naomi said, "a smart girl like you."

Ruth returned Naomi's brief smile, and they kept walking.

❧

Naomi stretched out her legs, trying to get comfortable on the hard wooden bleachers that weren't fit for anyone past a certain age to sit on. She was watching Sarah and a dozen other little girls learn to play tennis on one of the city park's courts. It was still a rich folks' game as far as Naomi was concerned, but Sarah swung that racquet like she thought she'd hit a home run or whatever it was called in tennis. She was better than most of the others; when one girl took a swing at the ball, the racquet slipped out of her hand and sailed over the net, clattering onto the court.

Naomi had become Sarah's primary caregiver and chauffeur since school let out for the summer. Eliza had lined up plenty of activities: tennis and 4-H on Tuesday and Thursday, piano and day camp at the Y on Wednesday and Friday, and a few outings with friends to the movies or to play putt-putt golf. Thankfully, Naomi had not been asked to shuttle anyone else's children. She'd driven the carpool routes with her own girls and didn't care to do any more.

Sometimes, like today, she would stay for Sarah's tennis lesson and join mothers, babysitters, and the occasional grandmother in the bleachers. Or she would watch the children in their swimming lessons at the Y, observing safely through the huge windows that separated the pool area from the main lobby. She had never learned to swim, and to this day she did not particularly enjoy even lounging by a pool. Lakes were fine as long as she didn't have to swim in them, and most lakes nowadays weren't fit to dip your toe into anyway.

Naomi watched the children slip in and out of the water like ducks. She'd given Evan a bath once and nearly had a heart attack when she lost her grip and water sloshed over

NANCY CROWE

his face. He spluttered a little, but forgot about it the next minute. Naomi wondered why God ever trusted babies to human beings. All it took was a moment of letting go or looking away, and they'd be gone.

Other times, she'd drop Sarah off and join the girls at Richie's. By nine-thirty Greta, at least, would be at the front corner table drinking coffee. It was the perfect place to see who came in and went out, or who stepped out for a cigarette since the diner now had a no-smoking sign ("Too many folks complained," Richie said with a shrug) in the window. Ever since another of their high-school buddies had died of lung cancer, none of them felt much like breathing in smoke anyhow. If you sat on the booth side of the table you could just see the bottom of the courthouse steps, and if you sat in one of the chairs you could see who went into Mimi's, the expensive ladies' clothing store across the street, or the windowless Masonic Lodge on the corner with the dark upstairs lunchroom where deals were made.

Lula usually joined them at Richie's, too, although she hadn't run with that crowd very much before. Naomi always figured Lula had better things to do than sit around drinking coffee with gals whose husbands didn't make a fraction of the money Lula's did. But she was a regular these days, and that was fine. Friends, especially the kind who knew how things were because they'd been there, were getting harder to find.

Greta had continued to teach Sunday school since the days when Marina and Cara were in her class. She'd have the kids act out Bible stories — even demonstrating the use of a real slingshot, to the dismay of the property committee chairman, in the David and Goliath story. Greta and Irvin, who was still alive although it was hard to tell, had only one child — a son who'd joined the Peace Corps and then decided to stay in Africa to teach. His mother just about busted a gut with pride, but the girls feared he'd be eaten by savages and never heard from again. "Wonder who'll take care of her down the road, in her old age," Lula often murmured.

Down the road, my ass, Naomi thought. Greta's face was just as animated as it had been when they literally ran into each other on their grammar-school playground. They'd briefly argued over who wasn't watching where she was going, and then Greta invited Naomi to her tree house and they'd been best friends ever since. But that was sixty years ago, and down the road could be tomorrow.

And now, of course, the girls were more interested in what had happened to Naomi. After all, she had left for San Francisco ten years ago with a husband and two daughters and returned with a young woman who wore a gold ring through her eyebrow. Naomi said, with as much brevity as she could get away with, that Marina and Cara both had job changes that made it necessary for them to move away and that Cara and her husband had split up after the baby died. If anyone asked about Ruth after hearing all that, Naomi said only that she was a friend of Marina's.

"That Ruth's a different sort, isn't she?" Lula said one morning.

Naomi's coffee cup froze en route to her lips. "How do you mean?"

"Well, she wears those boots, and those blouses that don't look like they were made anywhere in the United States. She wears all those jewels and dangly earrings, and the little doohickey in her eyebrow. And she sure has some funny ideas about what the law ought to be. She favors special rights for deviants." Lula dumped another packet of artificial sweetener into her tea.

"Lula, let's not start that again." Greta shook her head. "Things are just different where she's from. Naomi, you know that better than anybody after living out there."

"It's different, all right." Naomi said, and took a swallow of coffee. She had to change the subject, and fast. There was too much about Ruth, or Marina and Cara, that simply could not be said.

Fortunately, Richie appeared with a coffee pot in each hand. "All right, ladies, who had regular and who had unleaded?" he asked, even though he got it right every time.

Lula turned to him. "Richie, you've seen Belinda's new receptionist, haven't you?"

"Temporary receptionist," Naomi said.

"Sure, they've been in here a few times." He refilled Naomi's cup.

"What do you think of her?" Lula asked.

"I don't know. Seems real polite. Leaves good tips. What else is there?" He grinned, chubby cheeks pushing his glasses upward. Richie was just like his daddy, only heavier and sassier.

"Oh, aren't you smart. Go get me some more hot water." Lula shooed him away.

Greta picked up her cup again. "I think it's nice to have someone visit from so far away and give us some perspective. Sometimes I think there's just so much we don't know here, things we don't appreciate." Her gaze drifted to the window.

Lula frowned, and Naomi tried to think of something funny, or at least distracting, to say. They were the same old girls, as much as any of them could be.

Naomi drove with Sarah from the park to the ice cream parlor, a little white cinderblock shop which had been a gas station before she left for San Francisco and had gone through about three owners since. The walls were covered with crayon drawings and thank-you notes from area schoolchildren, interspersed with ads from the community theater and a couple of missing-child posters. Sarah opted for a scoop of German chocolate on a waffle cone. Naomi wondered how the ice cream stayed in the cone with that hole at the bottom, until Sarah explained that a piece of candy plugged the hole. Naomi had a scoop of fudge ripple in a little plastic cup.

"I can't believe we're having ice cream before lunch," Sarah said almost breathlessly, as if they had just rang someone's doorbell and then ran.

"You know what they say. Life is uncertain, so eat dessert first," Naomi said.

"Who said that?"

"I don't know, but they sure had it right about life being uncertain."

"Are you going to stay at Grandma's house a long time?" Sarah asked in between strategic licks to keep her ice cream from rolling down the cone in muddy rivulets. It was early July and almost too hot to sit at one of the round stone tables outside the shop, but they did anyway.

"Well, I don't know about that," Naomi said. "I suppose I ought to think about getting my own place."

"Grandma's house is big. You could stay if you wanted," Sarah said. "One time, my dad dropped me off really late at night when he had to go to work and Mom was at Grandpa's house. Grandma didn't even know I was there until morning. I walked down the stairs and said 'Hi,' and she jumped about three feet in the air."

Naomi laughed. "I imagine so, if she didn't even know you were in the house."

"Is Ruth going to stay, too?"

"I don't think so. She teaches school in California, and that's where she belongs."

Sarah tilted her head to one side. "What do you mean, that's where she belongs?"

"It's where she grew up, and her family and friends are there."

"You're her friend, too. Grandma's her friend."

Naomi scraped the sides of her cup for the last drops of ice cream. "Ruth's been real sweet to come all the way out here with me, and to help your grandma out at the office. But she's got to go back to her teaching and her life out there in San

NANCY CROWE

Francisco. This just isn't her kind of place."

"I think you both should stay." Sarah crunched her cone. "It's more fun since you got here."

"You think so, huh?"

"Yeah. I hear Grandma laughing a lot. Ruth, too. Uh-oh." A dribble of ice cream had escaped the cone and was on its way down her small wrist.

"I wonder what's so funny." Naomi instinctively dabbed at Sarah's wrist and mouth with the coarse paper napkin. She had noticed that Ruth and Belinda were spending a lot of time together outside of their working hours. Sometimes they went out for dinner or coffee after closing up the office, and wouldn't come home until ten or eleven. Apparently it was working well to have Ruth fill in for Belinda's receptionist. Belinda was a good influence on Ruth, who probably hadn't had near enough of that.

Lula, Naomi reflected, always did tend to go on like she knew more than she did, but there was generally some truth in what she said if you cared to listen long enough.

It would reflect badly on Naomi and the rest of the family if Ruth didn't have the decency to keep her mouth shut about certain things. To hear Lula talk, it already had. Naomi would be the one to blame for bringing back one of the worst things San Francisco was known for, instead of a little toy cable car or a framed poster of the Golden Gate Bridge. She should never have gone to San Francisco in the first place, and she didn't want anyone saying she should never have come back.

Especially Belinda, whom she'd had to get to know all over again. Each had known the other as part of the extended family package, but Naomi couldn't remember the last time the two of them really talked. They'd been born twenty years apart, and Belinda's family had had plenty of money for her to go to school and become a doctor. Everyone was so proud and all in a dither about having a lady doctor in town and in the family. Aunt Violet never missed a chance to talk about how well Belinda did on her exams or how bravely she'd withstood the work at that big university hospital, and then she'd sweetly ask what Naomi was up to these days.

Aunt Violet had been tight-lipped when Belinda and Griff split up. Naomi couldn't understand what had gone wrong. Griff was a nice man, and a successful one, and they'd known each other since they were kids. Nobody thought he had a lady friend. But by that time, most folks in the family and in town had developed a near-ironclad confidence in Belinda's judgment. She would come tend a feverish baby in the middle of the night or help an old man walk down the hall to the rec room at Autumn Glen just because she was there. She knew what people needed.

Belinda had been bringing coffee up to Naomi each morning before she and Ruth left for the office. Sometimes she pulled the chair out from what had been Eliza's homework desk and stayed to chat for a few minutes, and Naomi began to see why her patients loved her so much. She listened as if whatever you were telling her might make a difference in what she did or said next, that she would think about what you said. Belinda, with her graying hair and almost eight years' experience as a grandmother, had become two people in Naomi's mind — the smart girl everyone fussed over, and the intelligent, thoughtful woman who cared for everyone else, including her broken-down old cousin.

"Naomi!"

"I'm sorry, honey. What?" Naomi laid a hand on the child's shoulder.

"I said maybe Grandma and Ruth are talking about you, and that's why they laugh."

"Oh, you little monkey." Naomi tickled Sarah as she burst into giggles. "See if I buy you ice cream before a meal again."

"Aww. How about if we play Old Maid and I let you win?" They got up from the table.

NANCY CROWE

"Deal." Naomi prepared to give Sarah a high-five, as the child had shown her before, but Sarah took Naomi's hand instead, swinging it between them as they walked to the car.

Chapter Nine

Ruth tapped her foot to the twanging thump of the music at *Buffalo Gals and Guys*, where three uneven rows of patrons tried out the dance steps they'd just learned from a man wearing a white cowboy hat.

Local legend had it that *Buffalo*'s, a little brick building with a gravel parking lot just outside of town, housed a speakeasy during Prohibition. It had gone through a few more incarnations before standing empty for several years. Then along came Ernest "Tex" Whitman — who'd never set foot in Texas — with an entrepreneurial itch and a few extra dollars for renovation, and Buffalo's was born. Ruth had to admit the place had a certain ambiance, despite the animal heads courtesy of Tex's "baby" brother, a taxidermist, and chalky murals of ranch, rodeo and prairie scenes.

She and Belinda had closed up the office and gone to dinner at Pete Weimer's *Ribeye*, the town's only three-star restaurant.

"You told me New Bethlehem has a night life," Ruth had challenged her. "Let's see it."

And so they ended up at *Buffalo*'s, the nearest alternative being a sports bar with a large-screen TV and, according to

Belinda, more than its share of notations on the police blotter.

"Have you ever been to a place like this?" Belinda asked over the whine of the Hawaiian guitar.

Ruth grinned. "Not exactly." She took a sip of beer and dragged her attention from Belinda to the line of unabashed dancers a few feet from their table. They stomped, slid, and clapped more or less when they were supposed to, in a reasonably even mix of guys and gals. At the tables and bar sat couples of just about every age; two men played pool in the corner while their wives sat and talked, cheering when one of the men made a good shot. Four or five couples in their thirties had pushed three tables together and laughed uproariously every few minutes, all happy and settled and acceptable.

"This reminds me of a song about a 'hetero honky-tonk,'" she told Belinda. Their knees touched under the small round table. "It's kind of fun, though."

"It is, indeed." Belinda traced the side of the wine glass with her finger.

Neither moved away from the contact. They watched a mass collision erupt on the dance floor when someone's boot scooted the wrong way. Out of the corner of her eye, Ruth saw a woman in a Western-style satin shirt approach their table, and Belinda moved her knee and repositioned herself in her chair. The woman walked on by. Ruth fiddled with the collar of her silk blouse.

Belinda's eyes darted in every direction except Ruth's. "We don't have the selection of night spots out here that you do, obviously, and I've never been much of a bar person."

Ruth leaned back in her chair. "There was this one bar close to campus. Kids who were just coming out would go there trying to find out what being gay means. After a while they'd figure out that life goes on and you still have to study."

Belinda watched the dancers for a few minutes. "I've been thinking about your question. About there being any visible gay community here," she added quickly.

"I wanted to ask Will — the bookstore guy — but I was afraid I'd never get out of there," Ruth said.

Belinda smiled. "That was smart. I've never been part of a gay community per se. I see my community as my patients, my church, the mechanic who's worked on my car for years." She looked down at her hands, twisting a cocktail napkin in her lap. "And the town, I suppose. I don't know anything else."

Ruth studied her. "It must be comforting to know that people would really notice and miss you if you weren't there."

"That's true."

But did they know her? Did anyone in New Bethlehem or beyond fully appreciate her? The music droned to a stop and kicked up again; this time it was vintage k d lang. Ruth wanted to jump up and take Belinda's hands in hers. "Let's dance," she said instead. Her smile spread into a grin.

Belinda set her wine glass down a little harder than necessary. "Huh?"

"Come on. We can't sit on our butts if they're playing k d lang," Ruth said. She eyed the swarm of jeans and boots on the floor. It was another line dance. No partners, nothing to lose except maybe some dignity.

"You've got a point there." Belinda smiled. "Let's go."

They merged into the back line. Ruth picked up the steps easily, having done line dances at parties, but Belinda managed to stay half a beat behind.

"Guess I ain't got rhythm," she told Ruth.

"Oh, yes you do," Ruth replied over her shoulder. They had just turned and Belinda was now behind her. She forced herself to concentrate on keeping her own feet doing what they were supposed to do while her mind absorbed the fact that she was dancing alongside a doctor in rural Indiana, and she wanted to keep dancing until she met her halfway. Maybe more. They turned again. "See, you're getting it."

"How about that. I guess an old dog can learn a few new

tricks."

They jumped and turned again, and Ruth placed her hands on Belinda's shoulders from behind and leaned forward. "You're hardly an old dog, Belinda."

Belinda momentarily lost her balance, and Ruth steadied her. "Whoops." She blushed a little, but maybe it was the dancing.

Everyone paired up again for the next song. The two of them stood still, arms at their sides, as the dance floor stirred into motion.

"One more?" Ruth stepped forward. This was Belinda's turf, the town she had to live in and make a living in. If she said no, Ruth would accept it gracefully.

Belinda froze. "Gosh, Ruth, I don't think that's such a . . . "

"That's okay. Why don't we go get another drink or something?"

Belinda was about to respond when two women spun past them, dancing together with no self-consciousness whatsoever. They were in their late fifties or early sixties, one with a beehive hairdo that was beginning to topple, and their husbands were probably sitting at the bar. Ruth watched Belinda watch them, knowing an almost clinical risk analysis was under way.

It didn't take long. Belinda moved closer and circled Ruth with one arm.

Ruth smiled and took Belinda's hand. The music was something short of the polka she'd learned in gym class years ago, a lot of stepping and turning and trying not to bump into anyone. Both of them watched where they were going, and Belinda glanced to the right and the left without moving her head. Ruth, too, discreetly scanned the faces around them. If anyone looked at them funny, the dance would be over. After a minute or so, Ruth turned her attention to Belinda's eyes, which had ceased their monitoring. She stopped thinking about steps or obstructions.

When they returned to the house it was dark except for the entry hall light that Naomi had left on for them.

"She must be asleep," Belinda whispered as they tiptoed toward the stairs.

"I hope so. We missed our curfew."

Belinda laughed, prompting a giggled shushing from Ruth, and another when one of them stepped onto the creaky stair.

Ruth reached inside the doorway to her room and switched on the light. "Belinda, thanks. This was great."

"It was fun, wasn't it?" Belinda blinked a little at the light.

Ruth leaned against the doorframe. This house where Belinda had grown up and raised her own daughter, this high-ceilinged hallway where they stood looking at each other, had been here for years and would last for many more. It was like the town itself: unwilling to accept renovation without concerted effort, and yet a different place from the one Ruth and Naomi had entered, depressed and exhausted, a few weeks ago. Her heart shifted into overdrive.

"Well, I'll see you in the morning." Belinda took a step toward Ruth and then stopped as if she'd reached the edge of a precipice.

Ruth took Belinda's hand in both her own and held it there between them, nearly pressing it to her heart. "Good night."

Once behind the door, Ruth exhaled, and for a few minutes she could do nothing but lean back against the door. Belinda had drawn careful, distinct lines around her life in New Bethlehem, and Ruth's Californian heart had just been flattened. She'd walked right into quicksand with Marina, and damned if she'd do it again.

She kicked off her shoes. For half a second she thought about knocking on Belinda's door and offering to make some tea. They would share a few more stories and observations until the conversation drifted around to where they could begin to figure this out, if there was anything to figure out.

NANCY CROWE

Ruth pushed the thought away and sat down at the metal desk, turned around once in the swivel chair, then held her forehead in her hands. The last thing she needed was to face an open door, only to have it inevitably close.

⁓

Naomi had not been to church since returning to New Bethlehem, even though Belinda invited her every week. Then it came time for the picnic, which was apparently the highlight of the summer for some people, and Sarah asked Naomi to come. Everyone knew that casual attire was permissible on this particular Sunday with the picnic immediately following worship, but Naomi nearly made them all late because she couldn't decide what to wear. She finally settled on white slacks and a navy blue top cut like a sailor suit. Ruth told her she looked like one of the kids in *The Sound of Music*, and Naomi retorted that she'd rather look like one of the kids than one of the nuns.

While the organist played a prelude in the fruitless hope of quieting churchgoers before worship, Naomi insisted the hummus Ruth had made would be too garlicky for most folks and Ruth had better put a sign on it so they'd know what it was. Naomi's mother's potato salad recipe would have been a wiser choice, she was certain.

"Naomi, a little spice and seasoning won't hurt this town one bit," Belinda said with a wry smile, sitting on Naomi's other side. Ruth tried to catch Belinda's eye, but she was looking through her bulletin.

Naomi dropped the subject once people she knew, some she hadn't seen in ten years, began to recognize and greet her. Jim Foster introduced himself before taking his place up front. Little old ladies bent to hug her. Parents brought their children over, explaining to the kids that this was the lady whose daughter, Marina, had been their babysitter; or that this was the mother of Cara, who had been one of their aunt's second-grade pupils. Naomi held court right there in the pew.

And then came the picnic.

∿

A bee zoomed past Ruth's ear and circled back; she fought the impulse to swat at it. She was packed in so tightly between Naomi and Sarah at the rough wooden picnic table that she might swat Naomi instead.

She felt like swatting whoever thought of having a church picnic at the hottest time of the day in July. The air was as sticky as Lula Masters' cinnamon buns: "My specialty," she said, as the glaze pooled in sugary clumps on the plate. The bugs, at least, were enjoying this.

The church had reserved part of the park, a cluster of picnic tables next to a small gravel pit of a pond. Two tables shoved end to end had been reserved for the food: a tray of fried chicken provided by some committee or other, about five dishes of potato salad in varying shades of yellow, several bean salads, a plastic punch bowl of cut-up fruit suspended in syrup, and plenty of baked beans drowning in watery sauce. The desserts looked a little more promising; Ruth had seen at least one plate of brownies.

Ruth's bowl of hummus, with its surrounding triangles of pita bread, had barely been touched. "What's this crap?" she heard one man grumble, followed by a shushing reprimand from the woman next to him in line.

Ruth wiped the sweat from her forehead, dearly missing her cool, foggy San Francisco, where people not only recognized but appreciated something other than meat, potatoes, and green bean casseroles with fried onions on top.

The conversation floated across the picnic table, their breath the only breeze they were likely to feel that day. Maybe people had to be born and raised with this oppressive mugginess in order to tolerate it. Greta, with whom Ruth had chatted by the volleyball court about books, plants, and the environment until Irvin wanted to go home, had barely seemed bothered by the climate. Neither did Naomi, for that matter. Ruth had heard the newscaster's warnings that the elderly were especially vulnerable to the heat, but these two looked as fresh and comfortable as if they were on a screened-in porch with a ceiling fan. Their generation had been taught that ladies did not perspire, at least not visibly.

Ruth could hardly believe that she and Belinda had danced together — that she'd had the guts to ask and Belinda had the guts to accept. The song was just bouncy enough for two women to dance together in a straight bar without turning too many heads, but torchy enough not to be too safe.

In the days that followed, Belinda had spent more time on paperwork, keeping the exam and supply rooms neat, and even vacuuming the floor when she thought the mom-and-pop cleaning service hadn't been thorough enough. One evening after the day's last appointment, Ruth asked if Belinda would like to go for coffee, but Belinda said she had a lot of things to catch up on at home. Once at home, Belinda sat and watched television with Naomi. Ruth had stalked into the kitchen and scrubbed dried crud off a pan, then dropped it with a bang into a sink full of soapy water and other utensils.

Today, Belinda sat at the other end of the picnic table and talked with Jan Foster, the minister's wife. When her eye fell on Ruth, she smiled briefly and turned back to Jan. Ruth pulled at one of her earrings until it hurt.

Sarah took off to play kickball, but the absence of her tiny form didn't open up much space. Eliza talked with a fellow parishioner and co-worker who had stopped by their table, until the woman loped off to examine a child's skinned knee. Mark, who as usual had been listening and saying little, asked his wife if she wanted another soda. She accepted almost shyly, as if they were on their first date.

Jan and Jim Foster's young teenage daughter had also excused herself to play kickball. Older teens milled about, too old for the game and too young to even think of sitting with the adults. Ruth was beginning to feel too young to sit with the adults herself.

Belinda, after all, was chronologically two decades ahead of her. Though she had lived in this tiny Midwestern town for most of her life, she had a wealth of experience — marriage, motherhood, becoming a doctor, coming out in midlife, and starting her own practice — that Ruth could only imagine. Belinda could probably remember exactly where she was when Kennedy was assassinated; Ruth hadn't even been born. She had, no doubt, watched the Watergate hearings on television; Ruth learned about the scandal in a history class. Certainly Belinda couldn't see Ruth as anything more than a kid — nice to have around, but of no further importance.

"Talk with Sam Monaghan about that." Belinda's voice cut through the humid air. "Of all the lenders I talked to, he was the only one who really listened to what I wanted to do with the practice."

"I'll give him a call. Were you able to get a pretty good interest rate?" Jan asked. She was a bit younger than Jim, with an easy laugh and a graying head of blonde hair which she usually wore clasped behind her head in a barrette made of olive wood from Israel. She and Ruth often talked about California and culture shock; Jan had been born and raised in Pittsburgh, and she and Jim had lived in a "suburb of a suburb" near Los Angeles during his first pastorate. Ruth knew that she recently left her job with an advertising agency in a neighboring town.

"It was decent," Belinda said, "but that was a few years ago. One thing I know he'll ask is, how are you going to get started?"

"That's a good question." She moved her arms, which had stuck to the regulation vinyl tablecloth, with a slight grimace. "I know how to sell ads and concepts, but I've got to get some people on board who can actually put it all together." Her gaze wandered down the table. "Ruth, didn't you tell me you did some ad agency work?"

"Huh? Um… yes. For a small agency in San Francisco."

Jan's face brightened. "We'll have to get together. I could use another point of view."

Naomi waved away one of the hundreds of mosquitoes intrigued by her hairspray. "Better talk soon — she's gonna hightail it back out to California pretty quick."

"That's right," Belinda said. "She'll go back to San Francisco and forget all about us."

Ruth stared at Belinda, her face growing hotter even as a cold chill ran down her arms. Belinda looked away.

"Excuse me." Ruth stood up as gracefully as she could from the picnic table. "I think I need some more lemonade."

The church crowd had thinned; no one was at the drink table when Ruth went to refill her environmentally unfriendly disposable cup. The pale yellow liquid streamed over what was left of the ice. Tonight she'd call for a one-way airline ticket. Sure, she'd come to New Bethlehem on the rebound, but that was no excuse for being stupid. If Belinda thought that Ruth could casually brush her aside and forget about her, that was exactly what she'd do.

"Well, hi, Ruth." The Rev. Jim Foster refilled his iced tea at the other cooler.

"Hi." She managed a smile.

"This weather's not much like California, is it?" He fanned himself with a limp paper napkin.

Previous conversations and life histories blurred in her overheated mind. "When were you there?"

His gray eyebrows furrowed. "Let's see, that would have been about six years ago. We moved out there from seminary, then to Richmond, Virginia, and then here."

"Oh… right," she said. "What did you do before?"

He leaned a little closer. His eyes, behind the squarish frames, were a sharp, open blue — like a movie hero who'd successfully reason with the bad guys rather than conquer them. "I was the meanest financial services company vice president you could ever imagine. Got up at five, was in the office by six-thirty, didn't get home for dinner but two or three nights a week, traveled all over creation to close this deal here and schmooze those people there. I didn't listen to anyone, especially not to myself, and definitely not to God. I hired people and fired people and made secretaries cry. Are you horrified yet?" His lips twitched as if he were trying to conceal a smile.

"Am I supposed to be?"

"Well, I had a massive heart attack at age forty-six, and that sure as heck horrified me," Jim said. "Not to mention Jan and the kids, who'd all but forgotten who I was. So there I was in the hospital, flat on my back with tubes going in and out of me every which way, and God finally got my attention. It took me a while to follow through, but a couple of years later I started seminary."

"That's quite a journey." Ruth took a sip of the lukewarm lemonade.

"There's nothing like a good near-death conversion, but mine was pretty run-of-the mill. At least that's what one of my mentors used to say." He winked. "Now I'm going to quit gabbing, because you get to hear that every Sunday, and let's find out what else we have in common besides sunny California."

Ruth could not help but like this man. Besides, it was refreshing to talk to someone whose identity was not steeped in New Bethlehem, and with a California connection at that. They strolled along the worn dirt path that circled the lake, or pond, or whatever it was; the minister in his polo shirt and dress pants and Ruth in her tank top, shorts, and hiking boots. She wondered how it felt to believe, deep down in your soul, that you were speaking and doing the word of God.

"Ruth, what do you hope to do here in New Bethlehem? Aside from helping your friends?"

Ruth raised an eyebrow. Plenty of people in town had asked what had brought her here or how long she planned to stay. No one had asked what she wanted.

"That's a good question," she said. "I'm afraid I don't have a good answer."

He bent to pick up a stone from the bank. With a sharp sideways thrust, he flung it toward the water, where it disappeared with a plop. "I never could skip stones. How about you?" Ruth shook her head, and he looked out over the water as if it were something much bigger. "Why do you think you're here?"

She wished she had paid more attention to her father's conversations with one of his best friends, a philosophy professor. "I'm not sure what you mean."

"I mean — now, don't tell the elders about this," he cautioned with a wink, "but I see energy fields. It's something I picked up when I was recovering from my heart attack."

"No kidding? I listened to a talk on energy fields in Sedona a few years ago, but I don't remember much of it."

"That's what a halo is, if you ask me — someone's energy field. That first day you came to church with Belinda, I saw all kinds of things going on with yours," Jim said. They began walking again. "Did something painful happen in your life recently?"

"Yes. Well, not long before I came here." It seemed so distant. "My… girlfriend left." She glanced at him sideways.

Jim nodded. "I thought so. What intrigued me was the fact that there was so much positive stuff going on there, too. I sensed — and this is the Calvinist in me talking — that you're here for a pretty important reason."

Despite the heat, Ruth felt another cold chill. "Like what?"

They dodged around some kids chasing an errant ball. "That, I don't know. But it sure looks colorful," he said, turning to face her.

Ruth smiled. "Like a rainbow?"

"Could be." Jim rested his hands in his pockets. "Could very well be."

Chapter Ten

Belinda closed the office one Wednesday afternoon to finish pruning the hedges in her back yard and take care of a few other chores. Ruth dusted, vacuumed, and did a few loads of laundry. Naomi had taken Sarah to the movies.

Ruth trudged up the basement stairs with a basket of warm, clean clothes and began folding them in the living room. Through the window she could see Belinda clipping the hedges with surgical precision.

Ruth had always known what to say to a woman who interested her. There was no dearth of eligible lesbians in San Francisco, and eligibility was often subject to change with little notice. She'd meet someone, and coffee, a drink, or dinner would follow. Each tried to figure out where the other's head was, if only for the evening, the next morning, or the next weekend. No strings, one or both would say. A few weeks or months later, a string would invariably surface and Ruth moved on to the next no-strings attachment. It was the same with Marina, except that the string had taken longer to show itself, and its fraying had left Ruth speechless.

Now there truly were no strings. Now there was a golden thread, gossamer-thin but sturdy as steel, which had spun itself into a cloak that settled over her. It weighed almost nothing in the summer heat and held enough warmth to withstand an Indiana winter.

The back door opened and Belinda stuck her head in. "Did the phone ring?"

Ruth looked up. "No."

"Oh." Belinda shrugged. "Must've been Lula's." She closed the door again.

Ruth sighed. She finished folding the clothes, organized them into piles for each current inhabitant of the house, and took them upstairs in a white plastic basket. At least the laundry could be put in its proper place.

❧

Ruth sliced a tomato and then pawed through the paper bag full of home-grown zucchini Greta had brought from Irvin's backyard garden. There was no such thing as growing a little zucchini; you either got nothing or enough to give to your friends, family, and co-workers for weeks. Fortunately, zucchini would work in the salad she was putting together for dinner. It was the latest of several meatless dishes she'd made since arriving in New Bethlehem; Belinda liked her creations and Naomi managed to be polite most of the time.

She heard bare feet on the linoleum floor behind her. Belinda, showered and wearing clean shorts and a polo shirt, smelled of soap and jasmine. Ruth resisted the impulse to reach out and run her fingers through the still-damp hair.

"Um..." For Christ's sake. She was a grown woman and an English teacher. But she had Belinda's attention. "About what you said at the picnic, that I was going to go back to California and forget about... everyone here."

"Mm-hm?" Belinda took a large yellow salad bowl from the cupboard over the sink. "Good gravy, I'll have to wash this. It's dusty as the Sahara."

"Well, I won't. I mean, I couldn't forget how kind you've

been, or how cool a lot of the people in this town really are," Ruth said. She could feel Belinda watching her as she rinsed a zucchini.

"You're right. There are a lot of cool people around here."

Ruth turned off the water, patted the zucchini dry with a towel, and met Belinda's eyes. "I especially —"

They both froze at the sound of the doorbell. Ruth wasn't sure if she felt frustrated or relieved.

Belinda didn't look too sure, either. "I'll... get that." She bumped into a chair on the way out of the kitchen, fumbled with the lock on the front door, and opened it. "Well, look what the cat drug in."

Ruth watched through the kitchen doorway as Eliza came in with a tall, slightly stout man with thinning red hair and a big smile. "Dad didn't tell me he was coming to town today," Eliza complained good-naturedly. "He just showed up at the factory."

The man dropped a kiss on Belinda's cheek, and she gave him a quick hug. "What brings you here?"

"Oh, the usual. A deal I didn't know about twenty-four hours ago, up at the old McNeal place. We finally found a buyer." His voice filled the entryway. He wore a business suit and a striped tie that was bold enough to be interesting, but not distracting. He looked like he could sweep through a room or a house and convince you it was the best place to be.

"Well, that's good news. And you're here in time for supper," Belinda said.

He laughed. "That's what we were counting on. If we wouldn't be imposing, that is." He looked past Belinda at Ruth, who had ventured into the entry hall. "I'm Griff Boaz," he said, extending his hand. He had the appearance and aura of a man who missed nothing.

She shook his hand. "Ruth Greene. I recognized you from a couple of pictures."

"Ruth came with Naomi from California," Eliza explained,

"and she's filling in for Renee. She's keeping Mom from pulling her hair out." She briefly rested an arm on Ruth's shoulder. It was not a company gesture, but a family one.

"Of course. You said something about that a while back." Griff turned back to Ruth. "It sounds like you've been in all the right places at all the right times."

"She certainly is." Belinda pressed her hands together. "Well. Naomi and Sarah will be back any minute, and we were just throwing something together. Help yourselves to something to drink." She returned to the kitchen and her muffin mix. Griff and Eliza followed her, all three of them chatting as glasses were filled with ice and bottles clanked in the refrigerator. Ruth turned back to the cutting board, feeling like a guest again.

"It's too bad Mark can't join us." Griff fished a bottle opener out of the silverware drawer for his beer.

"I hate to have him working second shift," Eliza said, pouring diet soda into a glass, "but it's better than third. Let me show you what Mom and Sarah planted in the back yard." They took their drinks outside.

Ruth's head was still spinning when they all sat down to dinner. Sarah couldn't stop talking about the movie she and Naomi had seen, and related every detail to her grandfather. When Sarah turned to her mother with a story about a boy who decided to paint the windows at day camp, Griff chatted with Naomi about San Francisco, which he said he'd always wanted to visit.

Ruth watched the easy interaction between Belinda and her ex as they brought each other up to date on their jobs and what was happening in New Bethlehem. They acted like old friends, which she supposed they were; friends who had pushed through the bitter end of a relationship in one form and become family in another. Ruth had thought this only happened in lesbian circles.

As conversation swirled around them, Belinda leaned to-

NANCY CROWE

ward Ruth, who was sitting beside her. "Are you convinced, now, that this is a nutty family — such as it is?"

Ruth turned to look at Belinda, thoroughly enjoying her presence. "I pretty much knew that already."

They laughed, and Belinda lightly ran her hand along Ruth's arm before getting up for more muffins. Out of the corner of her eye, Ruth saw that Griff had noticed this exchange as he listened to Naomi describe the time her church women's group toured Alcatraz.

The doorbell rang shortly after they cleared the table. "This is a popular place tonight." Belinda said, and put down a stack of dishes.

This time it was a young mother who lived two doors down, on the other side of Lula. Ruth and Naomi had chatted with her a few times on their walks, and Naomi fussed over her eight-month-old baby. "I hate to bother you, but I think something's wrong with Mrs. Masters," she said. "I went over to get our mail... we just got back from Dick's mother's... and she seemed weird. Real pale. She just handed me the mail and shut the door in my face. You've known her a lot longer than I have..."

"I'll look in on her. Thanks, Sandy." She closed the door and walked slowly back into the kitchen. "Ruth, why don't you come with me?"

Ruth looked up from the muffin tin she was scrubbing. Why her? "Sure."

They excused themselves and walked next door in the dusk. No lights appeared to be on in Lula's house, an elegant, understated two-story limestone structure.

"What do you think's going on?" Ruth slowed her steps.

Belinda hesitated. "Like all patient information you deal with, this is strictly confidential."

Ruth nodded. "Of course."

"Her son John was one of my patients. He had to drop out of college — his parents cut him off when they found out he was gay. I don't think he and Lula have spoken in ten years. He didn't even go to his father's funeral."

Ruth paused to re-assemble the pieces of Lula she'd carried in her mind. "She said all those things about gays, and..."

"Exactly." Belinda sighed. "Anyway, he has AIDS." Ruth had seen that coming. "He's been living in Indianapolis, and his partner died last fall. A friend of his called a couple of months later and said John probably wouldn't live past Easter. And here it is late July." Ruth saw a trace of a tear.

"Oh, Belinda," she said. "So you think —"

"I could be wrong."

"What... what would you like me to do?"

"It's a variation on the buddy system. Just be there."

Lula answered the door wearing a shapeless pair of summer slacks and a ruffled blouse with the ruffles going in several different directions. Her face was as white as the picket fence around her garden.

"Hi, Lula," Belinda said. "How're you doing?"

She looked at Belinda, then Ruth, and back at Belinda. "John's gone."

"Oh, Lula, I'm sorry." Belinda hesitated. "May we come in?"

Lula allowed them to enter, and Ruth tried not to gape. The furniture had to be at least as old as the house, all curlicue patterns, gracefully curved table legs and tall chair backs. A collection of what appeared to be antique vases lined one wall.

Belinda put her arms around Lula and held her for a moment. Lula barely seemed to notice, but she allowed Belinda to guide her to a sofa upholstered in a shiny yellow fabric.

"Do you want to tell me what happened?" Belinda sat down with her.

Lula swallowed hard. "Some... friend of his called a little while ago and told me."

"Did the friend say what happened?"

124   NANCY CROWE

"He..." She pressed her lips together, and minutes passed before she could speak again. "He had that... disease." She looked at Belinda. "Did you know?"

Belinda flexed her hands in her lap and did not look up for a moment or two. "He told me he was HIV-positive a couple of years ago," she said finally.

Lula stiffened. "He did?"

"Yes, and of course I held it in confidence. I seriously doubt that anyone else in town knows."

Lula bent forward, her petite frame folding into itself. "I guess I always figured he'd get it."

Ruth perched on a nearby chair which looked like it should be roped off as too rare and antiquated to actually use. This scene had played itself out again and again in the living rooms of the friends and acquaintances she had lost to AIDS. It was the scene that didn't show in the ads for condoms and viatical settlements, in the public's consciousness of the disease and its prevention, or in the behavior that continued despite any and all warnings.

Lula looked at no one and nothing in particular. "I taught him everything. I tried to, anyway."

"Of course you did your best. We all do, with our kids," Belinda said.

Lula rose and began to pace the length of her Oriental rug. "I must have done something wrong for him to live like he did. And then to get sick and not even tell me."

"I know you loved him very much," Belinda said, "and—"

"Not enough." Lula's breath quickened with her pacing.

"He loved you, Lula." Belinda's eyes followed Lula back and forth.

"Well, he had a damn fool way of showing it." Then she noticed Ruth sitting on one of her tastefully preserved chairs. "I suppose this happens every day out where you're from."

Ruth sighed. "It happens too much. Everywhere."

Lula waved her off. "What the hell do you know." She

resumed her pacing.

"A couple of friends have died of AIDS in the past year," Ruth said. "One's parents were devastated. The other guy... his parents didn't even come to the funeral."

"Why should they?" Lula was crying now, her mascara smudging. "You live like that, you throw everything away." She stopped in her tracks and looked at Ruth.

A thousand responses crowded Ruth's mind. Slowly she stood up, trying to filter and edit them. Then Lula crumpled with a loud sob, and Ruth dove to catch her. She and Belinda got her back onto the sofa, where she sat in an uneven heap between them.

"Has anyone called Todd?" Belinda asked.

"I don't think he knows," Lula whispered.

Belinda went into the kitchen to track down a phone number for Lula's other son. Lula looked at Ruth through tears and smeared makeup, and Ruth put a box of tissues within reach.

"You must think I'm a miserable old fool. And you'd be right if you did."

Ruth shook her head. "Not at all." Both were quiet for a few minutes; Ruth heard Belinda's hushed voice on the phone in the kitchen. "I wish I knew what to say."

"That's all right," Lula said absently. "Why should you?"

Ruth could feel the older woman's tension as the news sank in that her son was dead and so was her chance to change anything. "What was John like as a kid?" she asked Lula.

"Oh, honey, he was the sweetest thing. He got beat up by the other kids so much I thought about schooling him right here at home. But then he grew a bunch and joined the basketball team. Nobody messed with him then." Ruth didn't doubt this; she had learned about the sanctity of basketball in Indiana. "I guess I should have worried when he didn't bring home any girlfriends." Lula sniffled. She seemed to study a spot in the middle of her polished coffee table. "And then..."

Belinda returned from the kitchen with a glass of water. "Here you go, Lula — I don't want you getting dehydrated on me. Todd and Becky are coming." Lula nodded, and Belinda thought for a moment. "I'm going to run home and get you something to help you sleep. I'll be right back."

Let me go get it, Ruth pleaded with her eyes; just tell me what and where it is. She started to rise from the sofa, but Belinda motioned for her to stay put.

"Can I get you some more water?" Ruth asked in the silence of Belinda's absence.

"No, thank you. I —" Her words were broken off by sobs.

Ruth gingerly touched the ruffled shoulder, and the older woman leaned on her. Ruth's eyes followed an arrangement of framed photographs on the wall over the piano, images of Lula and her late husband, a young man with a shiny-haired woman and three little kids, and the kids by themselves. It looked like Lula had only one son, and now she did.

They were still sitting like that when Belinda returned with a small pill, which Lula dutifully swallowed. Belinda and Ruth helped her upstairs to a master bedroom which could hardly be called a mere bedroom; bedchamber might be a better word. It stretched from the front of the house to the back, with heavy-curtained windows on three sides, a sitting area, and a fireplace.

"I don't know what..." Lula faltered, already drowsy as they eased her onto the king-size bed, where she looked very small and lost. Her eyes focused groggily on Ruth. "Thank you." Ruth squeezed her hand.

They waited downstairs until Lula's son and daughter-in-law arrived with sleepy children in tow, and didn't get home until after midnight. Griff, Eliza, and Sarah had long since left, and Naomi had gone to bed.

Belinda flipped the kitchen light on. The dishes were done and put away, the sink scrubbed, and the countertops spotless. Naomi had cleaned up and then some.

"If anybody asks, and I know they will," Belinda said, rubbing her back, "just say that John was very sick, and that's all you know. It's all anyone else needs to know for now." She turned the light off again.

Ruth agreed. "I hope she's going to be okay."

"I do, too." They walked toward the stairs, which were eerily lighted from the upstairs hallway. "Lula's a tough lady, but this is the second time she's lost John. She's going to need plenty of support and prayers."

"I know."

Belinda turned to Ruth. "Thank you for... tonight. I know it was hard, but... you were the one I wanted with me over there." She drew Ruth into a tight hug.

Ruth wondered if Belinda could feel how hard her heart was beating. Or maybe it was Belinda's. "Any time."

Slowly, Belinda let go. "Good night."

The funeral for John Edgar Masters was conducted at the church where he had been baptized and confirmed, his father had been eulogized, and his mother sat on the board of elders. It was a place where people filled the pews and gabbed in the basement year after year because they always felt it was the right thing to do, then came to realize they cared enough to show up anyway.

Naomi and Greta formed a two-member squadron around Lula, one of them always at the ready with a handkerchief or a cup of cold water. They sat right behind Lula in the front pew, which had been reserved for family. Ruth thought they all should have been in the front row.

Nothing was said about the circumstances of this man's passing; in fact, little was said about John himself. There were a few references to his high school basketball career and caring nature, but the rest could have been about anyone. Jim Foster, who had never met John, said some very nice things which nobody really heard anyway.

Ruth watched Jim mop his balding head with a handkerchief after the service as they prepared for the procession to the cemetery. What a thankless job, doing a funeral for someone he didn't know. Someone John's mother wouldn't have wanted Jim to know.

Belinda, Ruth, Naomi, and Greta drove to the cemetery in Belinda's car, right behind the hearse and Lula's family.

"John was a sweetheart, all right," Naomi said from the front seat, as the line of cars wended its way down Main, Ewing, and out Bram Road.

"He sure was." Greta adjusted her seat belt. Both Greta and Naomi had heroically donned pantyhose and dresses and carried purses that were appropriately impractical. Naomi's was a white leather clasp that only held her billfold, so she asked Ruth to carry her extra handkerchief and a compact in the pockets of her light cotton blazer. Greta had stuffed what she could into a little straw bag she said was the dressiest purse she had, but she kept checking to make sure it hadn't popped open or busted a seam.

"He worked in our nursery for a while, mostly weekends and summers," Greta said. "Irvin just loved him, teased him all the time. He was like another son."

"Honey, I don't remember him workin' there," Naomi said. "Was that before he went off to school?"

"Yes, and then when he came back after his first year. We even hoped he'd get a degree in botany or horticulture or something and take over the business when we were ready to retire. But he went for architecture instead, and we sold it to somebody else." Greta sighed. "We didn't hear much from him after that." She started to say something else, but stared out the window instead.

The plot was a good walk from the narrow cemetery road where they parked; whoever designed the cemetery had not done so with automobiles in mind. Ruth, Belinda, and "the girls" fell into step behind Lula and her son and daughter-in-law. Mark and Eliza joined a smattering of aunts, uncles, cousins, and friends who followed them across the damp grass, stepping around headstones and grave markers.

A white canopy shielded the inner circle from any rain that might fall from the clouded sky. Ruth saw many people from church, everyone wearing his or her Sunday best and a suitably stoic face. After the prayer, Jim invited each person to take a flower from the many arrangements surrounding the grave and lay it on top of the casket. Ruth, mindful of the thorns, chose a white rose tipped with lavender and added it to the pile of color.

Everyone walked back in the same loose clusters, only now Naomi and Greta each had an arm around Lula and it looked as if all three of them were holding one another up. Mark took Eliza's hand as they walked across the lawn.

They were about halfway between the gravesite and the cars when rain began to fall; preliminary drops, then insistent streams. The reverent walk turned into a rush for cover.

Ruth did not rush, but instead opened the rainbow-striped umbrella she carried and held it over Belinda and herself. She was ready.

Chapter Eleven

Ruth finished scheduling an appointment for an older woman with a sore hip, took Jan Foster off hold, and agreed to meet with her later in the week at Jan's home office, the beginning base for her ad agency. Jan, her voice pitched with excitement and dread, had some potential accounts and wanted Ruth's input. The two of them had already spent a Saturday afternoon poring over records, budgets, and designs for everything from business cards and brochures to actual advertisements. A couple of clients from Jan's old job had followed her with their faith and their deadlines.

Three or four calls had come in rapid succession, but the phone was now silent. The day's last patient had just left.

She found Belinda standing in the corner of her office by the window and bookshelves, and Ruth could not tell if she was looking at the lavender crystals or scanning the shelves. The white coat she put on only when she had to — such as when she visited her patients at the regional hospital half an hour away, as she'd done that day — had been tossed over a chair. Belinda wore a flowing blue batik dress she'd said Eliza had given her for Mother's Day.

"You look like you're on the trail of something," Ruth said.

"I'm trying to find an article, one of the first ones on AIDS to be published in a medical journal. Do you have any idea what year that might have been?" Belinda ran her finger along a row of journals.

Ruth thought for a moment. "Sometime in the early eighties, but I guess that doesn't help much." She watched Belinda pull a volume off the shelf and flip through it. "You must be feeling very sad about John."

Belinda sighed and turned a page. "The last time I saw him as a patient was when he came home from college at Christmas." She did not speak for a moment. "A few months later, he didn't have a home. Griff pulled a few strings to help him get a job in Indianapolis, and I looked into some scholarships and work-study programs. He did finish college a few years later. He sent me a copy of his diploma and drew a little watering can next to his name. When John was growing up next door, he was always getting after us about watering the flowers. Sometimes he came over and did it himself. Under the can he wrote, 'Thanks for everything. Love, John.'"

Ruth smiled. "That's quite an honor," she said.

"It is, indeed." She turned toward the window. "I didn't hear from him again until he stopped by a couple of years ago. He was thinner and his hairline was receding — this was the kid whose high-school sports injuries I bandaged up." She smiled a little. "He was on his way somewhere on business, and his mom didn't know he was in town. He told me he'd tested positive and that he was seeing a specialist in Indianapolis. I told him I wanted to be kept apprised of his condition, and I managed not to cry until he left."

Ruth felt tears well in her own eyes. "Did you always know he was gay?"

She nodded, and Ruth realized that of course Belinda knew.

"It's funny," Belinda said, "the things your hunches tell you about patients that all the diagnostic tools in the world don't. He may have guessed the same about me, even back when I was married." She shifted the volume from hand to hand. "I discussed condoms with him when he was a teenager. I keep thinking there's something more I should have done or said when he showed up at my office and told me his folks threw him out because he was gay. That's why I'm hunting down that article, because I can't remember exactly when all this AIDS stuff started." She replaced the volume and pulled out another.

"It's been an issue since I was pretty young," Ruth said, "but you shouldn't second-guess yourself. I'm sure you gave him the best care in the world, but the rest was up to him. For a while now it's been hard not to know about AIDS and how to prevent it."

"I know. A health teacher over at the high school wanted to include a discussion of AIDS a few years back, and they actually let her do it. There were plenty of restrictions, of course, but they wouldn't even talk about birth control when John was a student there." She put the volume back on the shelf and half-leaned, half-sat on the edge of her desk. "All doctors have to learn that they can't make everyone in the world better. Or everyone in town, or even in their own practice. It's been a very slow lesson for me."

Ruth stood halfway between Belinda and the door. The words wouldn't come, but they had to. "Belinda, you make a huge difference in the lives of so many people around here," she said. "I don't know why you don't see that. They're truly glad to see you, and there aren't many doctors you can say that about." She winced inwardly at the dangling preposition, but the train had left the station. "I wish you could understand, and maybe you already do but it's just not in a place in your mind that you can reach right now… but you would make people's lives better even if you weren't a doctor. It's who you are that makes a difference." She paused to catch her breath. "Especially to me."

Belinda held her gaze as though Ruth might disappear if she looked away. She put both hands on the desk. "Are you..."

Ruth closed the distance between them and slipped both arms around Belinda, pulling her to her feet. She tentatively kissed Belinda's cheek, temple, and forehead.

Belinda placed her hands on Ruth's shoulders. "Ruth, are you sure that... um..."

"Yes."

Belinda's arms tightened around her as she pressed her lips to Ruth's, lightly at first, then deepening into something so fine and rich that Ruth wasn't sure she deserved it. Belinda stroked Ruth's hair and kissed her again, and then her lips traced a path to the delicate skin around Ruth's eyes. In an instant, everything had changed; Belinda was different to her now. And yet she was the same. Ruth opened her eyes.

"Why me?" Belinda stroked Ruth's cheek and neck.

"Are you kidding? Why *me*?" Ruth laughed. "I'm the one who doesn't know corn from soybeans, and other vital life lessons."

"You know more than you think," she said as Ruth nestled into her.

"That's a scary thought." They held each other wordlessly for a few minutes. Ruth lightly touched Belinda's hair. It was ordinary hair, neatly cut and with the same proportion of dark and gray as the hair on thousands of heads, but Ruth wanted to finger each strand in the sun, to notice each glimmer and highlight.

"Where do we go from here?" Belinda asked.

"Where do you want to go?" Ruth ran a finger along Belinda's collar.

"Well, you have students waiting for you in San Francisco. Not to mention the rest of your life there," Belinda said. "And I have my patients and my family here."

Ruth held Belinda's hand as if reading her palm. "I don't know," she said after a long pause. "I suppose we can work

NANCY CROWE

around that."

Belinda sighed. "It's a long way. Neither of us can easily afford to hop a jet plane here or there for the weekend."

"I know," Ruth said.

"And then there's Naomi, and Eliza, and Sarah. And everybody else." She cupped Ruth's chin with one hand. "These are things we're going to have to figure out."

Ruth caressed Belinda's back, feeling the warmth of her skin through the fabric of her dress. How could she get rid of that sadness in Belinda's eyes? Belinda was allowing Ruth to step further into her life, far enough to make a difference.

"I'm willing to work on a solution." Belinda looked her in the eyes. "If you are."

Ruth's heart leaped forward. She drew Belinda to her. "Yes. I am." She closed her eyes against a tear.

"In the meantime," Belinda said, "Naomi's making meatloaf from the secret family recipe my mother all but took to her grave, and if we're late for dinner she'll have our heads."

Ruth wrinkled her nose. "That's not a very good solution."

Belinda laughed. "Definitely not." She kissed Ruth again, then stroked her hair and touched her face as if she couldn't believe she was real. "Let's go home."

And they did go home, to Naomi anxiously peering into the oven every thirty seconds, Eliza attempting to help and getting shooed away to set the table, Sarah gathering empty coffee cans for some backyard project, and Mark, off for the evening, on the floor trying to fix his mother-in-law's temperamental dishwasher. It was a kitchen full of people, chatter, and life. Belinda, who had been quiet — shy, almost — on the short drive home, quickly became absorbed into the fray as if she'd come from just another day at the office. Ruth watched from across the dinner table as Belinda tried to listen to Naomi and Sarah at once. Each person at the table would eventually go home or retire for the evening. But as the voices swelled around her, Ruth had a feeling that being alone with Belinda — not just by themselves, but in a place where the fears and concerns of others would not intrude — was going to be more difficult than she'd thought.

"Da — uh, darn it all," Naomi corrected herself, glancing in Sarah's direction and poking at the slice of meatloaf on her plate. "I don't think I got this quite right."

Ruth knew the feeling. "Well," she said, "you can always try again."

Chapter Twelve

Naomi shivered in the cool church basement and peered over Ruth's shoulder at the place cards for the women's retreat. "You spelled that wrong," she said, and shuffled through the pink registration forms again. This was the first time Lula had personally asked Naomi to help with any of her projects, and damned if she'd screw it up.

Ruth, sitting at one of the tables that made the basement a fellowship hall, frowned at the name. It took up most of the space on the dainty white card. She folded the card inside out and reviewed the list of attendees. "It seems like about eighty percent of the last names around here are German."

"You better believe it, honey. Jan Foster's coming, isn't she?"

Ruth ran her finger down the list. "She signed up, but she said something about a conference this weekend."

"Hmm. I remember when a preacher's wife didn't dare not show up for one of these things." Naomi looked around. "Where do you think we should put that big flower arrangement?"

Ruth finished printing the name. "I'd say up there, by the lectern."

"Good idea." She bent to pick up the huge pot.

"I'll get that." Ruth jumped in front of her and whisked it to the front of the room.

The daylong women's retreat was Lula's latest effort; she had recruited volunteers for the low-income day care down the street and collected used clothing for the homeless shelter in Waynesville. Plans for a bake sale were already under way. Naomi and Greta had together agreed that it was probably best to help when they could and get the heck out of the way when they couldn't.

Naomi watched Ruth tidy each fake-flower centerpiece, moving from table to table in jeans and a purple T-shirt from one of the festivals she'd been to out West. Her hair fell forward as she leaned over to smooth and tighten a ribbon; she pushed a tawny-gold lock behind her ear and looked at the centerpiece with one eye as if she were hanging a picture. It was funny the way Naomi had gotten used to Ruth's eyes being green one day, brown another — hazel was the right word. Now Naomi could have a whole conversation with Ruth and all she would notice about Ruth's eyes was that she was listening.

She'd been slouching less and smiling more, and she'd certainly been eating better in Indiana. Some time in the heart of the country, far from the craziness on the coast, must have been just what Ruth needed.

Naomi rubbed her back and slowly turned around. The basement had seen better days; the building committee needed to get off their duffs. She could still see and hear her girls clattering down those bare wooden stairs in the patent leather shoes she'd made them wear to Sunday school. Although she had left Belinda's address with her neighbor Lucia on Estancia Boulevard and with the post office in San Francisco, she had not heard from either daughter. She wondered which hurt more, losing a child to some mysterious syndrome or cancer like Cara and Lula had, or having them go away and stop speaking to you.

Naomi looked around at the brightly-colored bulletin boards decorated by the Vacation Bible School teachers and the "Prayer Concerns" cork board that lost more of its cork every week. Off to the right was a small kitchen with a pass-through for handing off bowls of soup or chili, casseroles in flimsy aluminum foil pans, or large trays of cookies or finger sandwiches. It was only a basement, and yet she'd probably spent more time here than in the sanctuary upstairs. Up there, if you were a kid you had to cross your little dangling ankles and be silent under penalty of spending the rest of the day in your room, or worse. Downstairs there were games and Bible lessons, songs and stories. She and Greta had been left to themselves in the basement one day when they were about ten; their mothers were upstairs sweeping the sanctuary or sorting donated shoes. When they got bored in the basement, they sneaked up to the bell tower and were shooed away by a hulking custodian only a little less frightening than the Hunchback of Notre Dame. They'd fled back down two flights of stairs and didn't want to leave the basement even when their mothers came to get them.

This was where a teenage Naomi had brought her brother and sisters on the nights when their father came home roaring like a tornado. You didn't know where the tornado would touch down or what might be broken, but you knew you'd better get out of its path. The church doors were never locked then, and they could come in anytime and read or play games. Always, Naomi asked her mother to come along; always, she refused. "He can't be here by hisself," she would whisper impatiently, as if her oldest child should know better.

Greta often joined Naomi and her younger siblings in the basement. Tall, loose-limbed and built like a boy even into her teens, she had long, shiny brown hair other girls would kill for and an imagination folks said might be the death of her. She'd duck behind the pass-through and entertain them with finger puppets formed from old gloves. Or she'd swipe a beard from the Christmas pageant costume box and pretend to be Moses. Naomi would shake a tambourine and play Miriam, and the kids were the Hebrews who just missed getting swept away after the Red Sea parted and then came crashing back together like the flood all over again.

She had stood at the foot of those stairs on that ungodly hot June day all those years ago, in her white wedding gown with the dramatic train her family couldn't afford but bought anyway. Her fine blonde hair had been pulled, wedged, and twisted into what she hoped would be a graceful upsweep, but in the end she'd just pinned it up the way she usually did in the summer. Dazed and overheated, she'd accepted best wishes as each guest came down to the reception. Greta, as she had upstairs, stood beside her in a flowing green gown as matron of honor. People always said they looked like Mutt and Jeff together, with Greta being a good five inches taller than Naomi, and she supposed they did even on that occasion.

"I have to go," she had told Greta through gritted teeth between greetings, "and you've gotta help me with my damn dress."

"Five minutes." Her friend did not turn her head or alter her smile. "You're the star of the show, in case you forgot. Can't you hold it for five more minutes?"

Naomi tried to glare at Greta while smiling at anyone else who might look her way. The result, Greta told her later, was an expression that made her look like a child trying to be scary on Halloween.

Ed, standing on Naomi's other side, had looked at them curiously. God, he'd been handsome in that tux; his face just glowed. "What are you two up to now?" he whispered.

"Nothing. Dear," she added. She turned back to Greta, who was supposed to be standing up for her, for heaven's sake. "I've been holding it all day," she hissed. "I'm telling you, I'm about to burst!"

"If you run to the bathroom now," Greta whispered, "everyone's going to think you're pregnant."

The fuss and formality of the day suddenly caught up with Naomi, and she could not stifle the giggles even when Ed's grandparents reached the foot of the stairs.

"Well," the grandfather said, taking Naomi's hand and patting Ed on the shoulder, "it looks like you're off to a good start."

They hobbled off for some punch, and then Naomi really did have to make a beeline for the bathroom. Greta, always there when it counted, went with her to help hold up her dress.

All the receptions that followed when the girls were baptized and confirmed had been held in this basement, and all the potlucks and other meals. God, they'd done more eating than praying. Lula had burned herself in the kitchen while heating up chili for a Sunday night supper, and she'd cursed so loud that her boys — they must have been in their teens — both turned bright red. Naomi had worked with Greta over the years to help dozens of children assemble miles of paper chains for Advent. Naomi had loved those workshops, kids everywhere and little pieces of paper getting glued all over the floor, but somehow everything was exactly where it should be. One such snowy afternoon, after everyone else left, Greta told Naomi she had miscarried. Naomi had held her as she sobbed. Greta never spoke of it again, but Naomi knew she still thought about it.

Greta's memory worked too well for anyone's good. She had stopped by Belinda's house a few evenings ago to give her the minutes from some church committee meeting or other. Belinda had gone to look at a softball injury, but Greta sat on the back porch with Naomi and told Ruth one story after another.

"A knife?" Ruth had sat up straight. "A cop caught Naomi with a knife loose in the car?"

Greta nodded. "That poor officer didn't know what to do. You'd think he would've seen it all before."

Naomi had not thought about that night in years. When she was in high school, her preacher uncle had loaned her his car to take some old Bibles to a Baptist family in Waynesville who were about to leave on a mission to some hot and buggy place. Greta and another friend, Evalene, went along to help. They delivered the Bibles and took the bulky black car up to the lake for a picnic.

"Naomi brought this loaf of bread that was just as stale as old money," Greta said, "and she knew how tough it would be to slice, so she swiped her mother's butcher knife and wrapped it up and stuck it in a bag with the bread. Well, it didn't quite make it back into the wrapping, or the bag. On the way home, this police officer pulled her over for speeding and ended up searching the car. He found that big knife under the seat and looked at her like she was Jack the Ripper."

"Evalene'd had so much wine she didn't know her fanny from third base," Naomi said. "She wouldn't even put out her cigarette to talk to the officer."

"Bless her heart, she was chain-smoking even then." Greta shook her head. "Anyway, the officer asked Naomi what she was planning to do with this knife, and she said she was planning to put it back in the drawer before her mother missed it. She even dug out a piece of that bread and tried to tear it in front of him, like she was serving the Lord's Supper, to show him why she needed the knife." She and Ruth both laughed like hyenas.

"And you just stood there with your mouth hanging open like he'd caught you holding up a bank," Naomi said. She turned to Ruth. "That's probably illegal now, him nosing through the car like that. It could have been illegal then, for all we knew. When I explained and he found out the Presbyterian preacher owned the car, he said he wouldn't file a report if I'd promise to be more careful with knives and drive a little slower."

Naomi sat back in her chair, listening to the crickets and cicadas try to out-sing each other. She could not recall ever hearing cicadas in California, but maybe she'd forgotten to listen. She had missed these Indiana summer evenings that smelled of dirt and honeysuckle, when she knew every sound she heard.

"Naomi was lucky," Greta continued. "Not like the time she soaped the teacher's window when she was about twelve, and got caught because her dress got snagged in the gate."

"Oh, you hush." Naomi reached across Ruth to slap Greta's knee. "She had it coming and you know it."

"And the time she forgot to put Ed's car in park and it went rolling down Hartford Street just as the factory was letting out."

Ruth laughed. "As flat as it is here, that's quite a feat."

Naomi looked from one to the other. "I oughtn't to leave you two alone, but I believe I'll get us a pitcher of iced tea. Greta must be dried out from all that talking."

They were still out there gabbing and drinking iced tea when Belinda came home; she'd stuck her head out the back door and asked what was so funny. Naomi realized then that she hadn't laughed so hard in months. For a good part of the summer she had no longer been in San Francisco, but she wasn't quite in New Bethlehem, either. The part of her that knew when she was home had crawled across the country, stopping at nowhere before she finally arrived.

Now Naomi turned her attention back to Ruth, who surveyed the crepe paper, tape, and fake flowers they'd spread out on the table. Ruth walked slowly around the room, paused to look behind her and then just above her eye level, tapping her fingers on her chin. Here was this girl, not even family or connected by anything that mattered anymore, who'd traveled all this way with her.

"What do you think about this stuff?" Ruth held up two

rolls of crepe paper, one pink and one white. "I think it's a little too much, especially with this low ceiling and the way the beams are spaced. But I'll put some up if you want."

Naomi walked to the center of the room, cocking her head to one side. "No, I think you're right. That would make it look like a wedding reception or... or a lunch for a bunch of little old ladies. Which it is, but we don't have to flaunt it." She smirked.

Ruth laughed. "Naomi, I think you have it in you to be an OOW."

"OOW. Oow? I give up. What is it?"

"Outrageous older woman."

Naomi burst into laughter. "Well, my stars. I think I'll take that as a compliment."

Ruth took a long piece of white crepe paper, draped it over Naomi's right shoulder, and taped the ends together over her left hip like a Miss America sash. "You should."

Chapter Thirteen

For three days after Ruth and Belinda spoke of their feelings for each other, they had not been able to steal more than a moment or two alone together.

Part of the problem was that everyone in New Bethlehem had managed to come down with an ailment or injure some body part that week. And Eliza and Sarah were in and out of Belinda's house even more than usual, or maybe it just seemed that way.

Then there was Belinda herself. Thursday night, after Naomi had gone to bed, Ruth came up behind Belinda in the kitchen and put both arms around her waist. Belinda turned around, apparently delighted, and they made out like teenagers for several minutes before Belinda broke away, her face a jumble of expressions Ruth could not decipher, saying there were some charts she had to review before the next morning's hospital rounds. Ruth was left standing, bewildered, in the kitchen, wondering if Belinda had changed her mind. Would she claim, as Marina had, that she never really wanted to be with Ruth in the first place?

After a family dinner Friday night, with everyone squeezed around the old fiberglass table on the back porch, Belinda reached over and took Ruth's hand. They held hands under the table until Sarah and Mark jumped up to chase lightning bugs in the yard. The tiny creatures darted and floated through the air, blinking their yellow lights as if to tease the father and daughter who gently caught and cupped them in their hands, watched them through loosely closed fingers, and let them go.

Naomi wanted Ruth to attend the women's retreat with her on Saturday, but she gracefully declined. Instead, she dropped Naomi off at church, borrowed her car, and drove away from town along a few country roads, past farmhouses and huge fields of green corn. Driving, when she wasn't caught in Bay Area traffic, had always helped her think. There was something about the motion and the need to focus on the task at hand that set another part of her mind free.

She dimly recalled passing the entrance to a state park on the way to New Bethlehem with Naomi. Sure enough, there it was. She paid the fee and wound through the park's narrow roads, wondering how the terrain could be so hilly just twenty miles from flat New Bethlehem.

Ruth parked the car and took the first path she found into the woods, wishing she'd thought to bring bug spray. Trees rustled in the summer breeze, more so far above her head where the branches swayed. These were not the evergreens of her beloved West Coast but a population of maples, oaks and others she couldn't even begin to identify. She stepped carefully on and across stones, watching for slippery ones that hadn't quite dried from the early-morning rain, and over roots. Belinda was right; the distance between them would be difficult to manage. There was no arguing with that. Or with the fact that Ruth had already come too far to turn back.

After about half a mile, the path opened onto some rocks above a stream rushing with the recent rainfall. She followed the stream for about half an hour, concentrating on her breathing and the pebbly path in front of her, until the stream wid-

NANCY CROWE

ened into a tributary of some river or other. Naomi had told Ruth its name, and probably the story behind the name, but she had forgotten.

She climbed atop a warm, smooth rock jutting over the water and sat down, dangling her feet over the edge. One wrong move and she'd be bumping down a rocky path into the river.

You shall rise up with wings as eagles. That was in the Bible; Jim had preached on it a couple of weeks ago, but she didn't recall it from Sunday school. He had spoken of God as a bird who catches faltering fledglings on her wings and carries them where they need to go.

As a child, Ruth thought her mother feared nothing. Ruth had sat in the back of countless courtrooms after school, watching her mother defend people who had no one else on their side, going up against big business and big government alike. She'd faced that jury as if she had absolutely no chance of losing, and she didn't lose very often. Outside of courtrooms and boardrooms, it was the same. Patricia Greene seldom lost, but the accomplished civil rights attorney who ate corporate bigots for lunch could do nothing about the way her daughter was treated in church.

Ruth drew her legs up and rested her chin on her knee. It would be nice to climb a mountain as if she had little chance of falling due to shifting rock or her own missteps. She closed her eyes, trying to imagine Belinda at the top of the mountain, but could not. Instead, Belinda climbed beside her.

Finally she dismounted from the rock and made her way down to the water's edge. She saw a flat stone on the ground and picked it up. Eliza had given her a couple of pointers on skipping stones; Ruth brushed off some sand and dirt and tried to remember how to aim it so that it would bounce over the water.

A cry from above sent Ruth's heart into her throat. An eagle, its wings outstretched and unmoving, made a long swoop over the water before flying out over the trees.

Ruth forgot about the stone and stood perfectly still be-side the stream. She concentrated on her breathing as she had on the path, trying to get the rhythm back, and on the sound of the water running steadily over the rocks. Soon a quiet calm settled over her. It was simple, much simpler than she might ever have allowed it to be.

∽

Belinda's car was not in its usual place. She must have gone to the retreat later, or maybe a patient had an emergency.

She sat down at the electric typewriter at the end of the dining room table. Someday she'd talk Belinda into getting a home computer. It took only one draft to write the letter, which she walked to the corner to mail. In the afternoon sunlight, Ruth dropped the envelope into the hot, dark mailbox.

∽

Belinda had gone to the regional hospital to visit a few patients, ended up scrubbing in on a delivery, and didn't get home until evening. Naomi had told Ruth every detail about the retreat and who said what, and she repeated it all for Belinda.

It was after eleven-thirty by the time everyone was in bed, but Ruth waited a little longer just to be sure. She tiptoed down the dark hallway, feeling like a fugitive.

The feeling dissipated once she had stepped inside the master bedroom and closed the door behind her. After tossing her T-shirt somewhere in the direction of a chair, she climbed into bed beside a quietly snoring Belinda. Ruth realized how tired she had been and was careful not to wake her. It was enough to be near Belinda, to feel her warmth and hear her breathing.

Belinda shifted in her sleep and turned over. In the light that crept in from the streetlight and glowed from the digital alarm clock, Ruth saw Belinda's eyes open, blink, and focus.

"Ruth?"

"You were expecting someone else?" Ruth teased, slipping an arm around her. She kissed Belinda, as delicately as air, savoring the jasmine fragrance of Belinda's shampoo, the musky scent of her skin, and the freshness of newly washed sheets. Fully awake now, Belinda drew in her breath as Ruth unbuttoned her pajama top. Her lips traveled down Belinda's neck to the smooth hollow of her throat and across where the sun had lightly browned her skin last week at the park pool. Ruth sensed Belinda's heartbeat quickening, felt Belinda's fingers rake through her hair. She retraced her kisses, working her way back up along shoulder, cheek, and temple, and looked Belinda in the eyes. The eagle brushed Ruth with its wings before circling back. "I love you."

Belinda caressed Ruth's shoulders, then her face. "I love you, too."

A beam of warmth ignited in Ruth's chest and spread through her, and she and the eagle took off over rocks, water, maybe even land.

"Am I going to wake up in the morning and find out none of this happened?" Belinda asked wryly.

"No, it's real." Ruth kissed along Belinda's hairline.

"I guess that's why I've been so skittish the last couple of days," she said. "A part of me still doesn't want to believe this is real."

"It's as real as you or I," Ruth said. "Why wouldn't you believe that?"

She twined a strand of Ruth's hair around her finger. "We... still have some details to figure out about the future."

"God is in the details." Ruth reached under Belinda's open pajama top to caress her back. "I saw that on a T-shirt or bumper sticker."

"And I think it's true." Belinda hesitated. "But... I think we should talk about that and make some decisions. Soon." She yawned. "I'm sorry. I've been up since six, drove half an hour to see three patients in the hospital, one of them very cranky, consulted with an even crankier orthopedic surgeon, and delivered a baby to top off the day."

"We can talk about it tomorrow." Ruth fingered a strand of Belinda's hair, then ran her hand over Belinda's shoulders and collarbone as if to memorize her. It would take the rest of their lives for her to fully appreciate this woman, and she looked forward to every minute.

"Well, maybe you can just tell me if there's a demand for general practitioners in San Francisco. I know everything costs more out there, and that would certainly include insurance," Belinda mused.

"You'd move?" Ruth raised her head.

"It's one option."

"I have no clue about insurance, but please don't go to San Francisco."

"Why not?"

"Because I don't have a job there. I've resigned from the city college," Ruth said.

An almost audible pause followed. "You..."

"I've given my department chair notice. Classes don't start for another month and my field is kind of oversupplied, so they shouldn't have much trouble finding someone to teach my classes. Jan Foster has all but offered me a job with her new agency. If she can't pay me right away, I'll find something else until she can."

Belinda sat up. "Ruth, are you sure this is what you want? It's... going to be a major change for you."

Ruth, too, sat up. She took Belinda's face in her hands. "It's already been a major change. I've thought this through more than anything I've ever done. I'm lousy at making decisions, and I've made some pretty bad ones in my life, but I think I've learned from each one... even if it's taken this long." She smiled. "I've always thought short-term, because I never could let myself see any further." Her fingers combed through the soft gray near her face and the darker strands in back. Belinda's eyes were barely visible, but Ruth needed no light to see the hope there. "I want to grow old with you, and I don't care who gets old first."

"At the rate you're growing in wisdom, you just may beat me to it." Belinda maneuvered Ruth back under the covers. She was quiet for a while. "I used to come home after these twelve- and fourteen-hour days at the office, sink into the living room couch, and try to forget that the world existed. Including myself." Ruth kissed her lightly. "Now... I want to exist."

Ruth blinked back a tear. "I'm certainly glad to hear that." She snuggled against Belinda's shoulder. "What are we going to tell Naomi and everyone else?"

Belinda tried, but failed, to stifle a yawn. "Gosh, I'm sorry." She sighed. "I think we should take that very slowly and carefully. It won't be easy. In fact, it'll probably be damned hard."

"I know."

She kissed Ruth's temple. "We'll work it out — I promise you that. They've got to get used to it eventually." Belinda's eyes looked almost bruised in the faint light. If Belinda needed space to sort out whatever baggage she might have checked through on this trip, Ruth would have to respect that.

"Do you want me to go now?" she asked quietly.

Belinda met Ruth's gaze. Slowly, she moved so that the length of her body lay against Ruth's, and tightened her arms around her. "No."

Some time later Ruth lay still, listening to a sleeping Belinda's heart and wondering why either of them had been afraid, and soon slept as well.

"Belinda?"

The sound poked through the fog of Ruth's slumber. She raised her head from Belinda's shoulder. "Wha…"

Belinda's eyes flew open, and Ruth felt her body tense. Daylight peeked around the curtains. Where was her T-shirt?

Another knock. "Belinda, honey, I can't find those coffee filters. Where'd you —"

Light from the hallway spilled across Ruth and blinded her as she tried to cover herself with the sheet. Her eyes adjusted in time to see Belinda do the same and to see Naomi's silhouette freeze, then back out of the room.

As quickly as the door had opened, it closed.

The Gate

Chapter Fourteen

Naomi turned and walked down the stairs as fast as a slightly arthritic knee would allow. It couldn't be. It just couldn't be.

In the kitchen, she filled a glass with water, gulped all of it down, and slammed the glass down on the counter. Her hand trembled and she willed it to stop.

"Naomi…"

She jumped. Belinda stood in the doorway in her worn terry-cloth robe.

Naomi could not look at her cousin. "I want her out of here."

"Now, wait just a minute —"

"I said I want her gone!" Naomi flung the glass across the kitchen, where it shattered against a cabinet.

Belinda ran a hand through her tousled hair. "Naomi, I understand that this is… something of a surprise. But you did barge into my room."

"What else has she done to you? What else has she done to this family?" Naomi demanded.

"Ruth has done nothing wrong."

"The hell she hasn't! Belinda… goddamn it." Naomi turned

away again. "You were supposed to be the smart one in the family. The one who did good all the time, for God's sake."

"Naomi, you need to calm down. Then you and Ruth and I can sit down and talk about this." Belinda had twisted the belt of her robe into something that looked like a deformed rattlesnake.

They'd all but lined up at the door, Ed, the girls, Evan, and her brother and sisters and mother and father before them, slipping out one by one. Belinda was still here, but she was no longer real. "No, we will not sit down and talk about this." She pushed past Belinda and grabbed her purse from the small table by the door. "I want her out of here by tonight, and if she isn't gone, I will be."

"This is my home." Belinda's voice rose. "And I want her to stay."

"Fine. You go to hell. I guarantee you will." Naomi slammed the door behind her.

She yanked the handle of her car door; it was locked. She'd had to lock her car, apartment, and everything else in San Francisco, and it had become a habit. Thank heaven the keys were in her purse, so she didn't have to go back in there.

Naomi roared down Belinda's street and onto Main with no idea where she was going. The traffic light at Main and Bertram, which had been a two-way stop before, turned red and she stopped with a jerk, looking blankly around her. Maybe it wasn't Main Street, after all. She was lost in her home town.

It was her own fault for bringing that bad element from San Francisco. It would have been better for Naomi to make the trip alone, even if she never arrived. But Belinda — what the hell was she thinking? Naomi banged her fist on the steering wheel, drawing a startled glance from the young man in the car next to her. It wasn't good for her to get so riled. She'd have to calm down.

The light turned green and she took off, tires squealing. It was evil, just plain evil. To have let that girl in her home and not done more to get her out of Marina's life — for that she deserved to lose both daughters and her grandson. She'd blinded herself and was paying for it, but she would be blind no more.

❧

She used to have a key to Greta's house, a brick ranch just behind the nursery that Greta and Irvin had tended all those years, but must have given it back when she moved to California. The grass in front of the greenhouse had not been mowed for a good two or three weeks, and a weed or two poked through the walkway. What kind of advertising was that for a nursery? It must break Greta's heart every time she pulled into her driveway. The place belonged to someone else now and there wasn't a thing she could do about it.

Naomi got out of the car and stretched, lacing her fingers together over her head. She had been driving around all day like some homeless person, which she supposed she was. Belinda'd made her choice, and there was nothing left to do but go back and get her things when no one was home.

The aroma of what was probably Greta's chicken and dressing, doctored up with whatever herbs Greta had growing, wafted onto the front step. It was one of Naomi's favorites, but she had not eaten all day and didn't think she could.

Greta opened the front door. "Well, there you are. We missed you in church." Her brow furrowed as she looked at Naomi. "What's the matter?"

"My own cousin kicked me out."

"What?" Greta moved aside. "You better come in. I think this heat's made you delirious."

Naomi followed her through the living room. Irvin was stretched out in that ratty recliner he'd had since they got married, watching some black-and-white war movie on television.

"Hey, there, Naomi." He barely looked up.

"Hey," she grunted in return.

Greta fiddled with the oven, fixed two glasses of iced tea, and joined her at the small kitchen table. The story tasted like bitter water as Naomi told it, something she'd taken a deep drink of before realizing it was poison. Greta listened like she always had. Every now and then she asked a question and it all came bursting forth again. Naomi lost track of what she had already said and what she still wanted to say; the details and points lay scattered like pieces of a child's board game shoved onto the floor.

"Are you sure it's... what you think?" Greta asked.

"I saw it." She rubbed her eyes. "I just can't believe Belinda would get mixed up in something like this."

Greta took a few more sips of iced tea. "Belinda's been my doctor, and my friend, for years. I couldn't have got through my heart surgery last fall if it hadn't been for her."

"Friends like that you don't need." Naomi felt the tears start again. "Someone like that has no business trying to make anybody well."

When Irvin strolled into the kitchen, she glanced at the clock over the stove; it was half past eight. She stared blankly out the window and realized she hadn't noticed the sun sink behind the trees on the other side of the nursery.

He leaned against the counter. That wayward curl of hair still drooped over his forehead, only now it was gray and there wasn't much hair around it. "Are we having supper sometime tonight?" he asked his wife.

Greta glanced from one to the other. "I'm sorry, hon. We just got to talking." She jumped up to check the oven, leaving Naomi alone at the table.

"Well, even Jesus and the disciples took time out from solving the world's problems to eat." He smirked. Irvin never smiled; he just smirked. "Even those hard questions like who gets to throw the first stone."

Naomi drew in her breath, but he just brushed by her and

went to wash his hands at the sink. Greta quickly set three places, darting around her husband on her way from the silverware drawer to the table, and dished up the food. Irvin said barely two words to Naomi. Five, if you counted "Pass the pepper." Greta tried to engage both of them in conversation, but they each ended up speaking mostly to her. Naomi always figured Irvin had so little to say that whatever he did say had to be delivered with a sting. It was no way to act toward someone who'd seen what she'd seen, and been cast out for seeing it.

Greta loaned her a nightgown and found her a brand new toothbrush in a shoebox under the bathroom sink. Naomi lay in their son's old bedroom, staring at the glow-in-the-dark stars and moons on the ceiling. Your own husband was one headache, but someone else's — even your oldest friend's — was quite another.

❧

In the morning, when she was sure that Ruth and Belinda had left for the office, Naomi retrieved her belongings and threw them into the car. She had a few boxes and pieces of furniture in Belinda's shed in back, but they'd just have to stay there until Naomi found another place for them.

From a pay phone outside the drugstore, she called Eunice Christiansen. Eunice had moved to New Bethlehem when her husband came to work for Wiggins Driveshaft; they'd bought a big old farmhouse out on Road 15 and rented out the land. Now her husband was dead and her children and grandchildren lived far away.

Naomi had helped Eunice out with a few carnivals and fundraisers when the girls were in school, so she didn't feel too bad about asking her to share some of her space for just a little while. She told Eunice she couldn't stay with her cousin anymore, and why. Eunice, once she could speak again, said there would be a hot cup of coffee and a comfy chair waiting for Naomi just as soon as she could get there.

Chapter Fifteen

Greta sat on the examination table, classy and ladylike even in a shapeless paper gown, while Ruth replenished the tongue depressors, cotton balls, and rubber gloves on the counter. Belinda was on the phone in her office with the door closed and had been running uncharacteristically late all day.

"Is it getting hot out there?" Ruth asked, standing on her toes to place a box of gauze pads on the top shelf of the cupboard. She had discovered that in Indiana, almost any awkward silence could be dissipated with a question or comment about the weather.

"Not too bad." Greta tugged at one of the paper sleeves and looked at the floor. She was in for a regular checkup, but Ruth hoped she wasn't sick. She closed the cupboard and was on her way out the door when Belinda came in.

"All right, let's have a listen." Belinda forced a smile. She fumbled ever so slightly with the stethoscope, and Greta pretended not to notice. Ruth shut the door behind her.

After Greta left, Ruth went back to the examination room. Belinda sat at the small desk, facing the window as if she were gazing outside, except that the window was shielded by a light beige curtain. She looked up and motioned for Ruth to close the door.

"Naomi's been talking," she said when Ruth sat down.

Ruth let out a long sigh. "I should have known."

Belinda turned on the stool to face her. "Apparently Naomi went to Greta's house on Sunday and stayed the night, but she and Irvin never did get along too well, so she decided to stay with Eunice Christiansen instead. Naomi and Eunice together are a gold-medal gossip team."

"Shit." Ruth sat back in her chair. "What do we do now?"

"I don't know." She stood and walked to the window. "Greta hasn't said anything to anyone, and she won't. She hesitated to say anything to me, but she felt she should warn me."

And me, Ruth added silently, but perhaps she didn't count.

"In the meantime, I no longer have a nurse." Belinda turned from the window and began tidying up the room, which was hardly in disarray.

"What?"

"Charlene quit. She said she won't work with perverts."

Ruth looked at the woman she loved, bent over the counter and on the verge of tears. "Maybe it's just as well."

❧

When they returned that evening, Eliza's compact station wagon sat in the driveway and its owner sat fidgeting at the kitchen table. Belinda set her briefcase on a chair, and Ruth saw the color drain from her face.

Eliza did not look up. "Ruth, would you excuse us, please?"

Ruth looked at Eliza and back at Belinda, and then no one looked at anyone else. "I'll be upstairs," she said.

She heard nothing until she closed the door of the catch-all room and sat down at the desk. Why had she come upstairs like a child sent to her room? She could have gone to the back yard, out for a walk, or into the basement to do some laundry. Anyplace would be better than sitting behind a closed door, listening to voices from the kitchen rising and falling in the same labored breath.

Belinda was downstairs explaining herself to her daughter, who was only two or three years younger than Ruth but had been an eyewitness to much of Belinda's history. Eliza could inflict pain, could drive in a wedge that Naomi never could. There was nothing Ruth could do, but perhaps she had done enough.

⁓

Ruth hung up the phone and exhaled, trying to expel what had just crackled over the line and into her head. At seven-thirty in the morning, a longtime patient had seen fit to call the office and say that she would rather see her daughters dead than to ever let them near Dr. Boaz again.

Ruth wanted to use the answering machine to screen calls, but Belinda would not hear of it. Her patients had almost always been able to connect with a live person right away when the office was open, and she did not want to change that.

"If you hear one nasty word, though," Belinda said, "you can hang up. With my blessing."

Seven patients had removed themselves from her care over the past two weeks, and she focused on the ones she had left with an almost military single-mindedness. They went to work early in the morning; Belinda had to manage without a nurse, and she put off looking for a replacement. She had not said a word about her conversation with her daughter, but Eliza had not been seen since. Sarah, Mark, and Naomi had all but disappeared too, which was nearly impossible in a town like New Bethlehem.

Having buried herself in work and battened down her emotional hatches — which, Ruth realized, Belinda had done for most of her life — little energy was left. Her conversations with Ruth did not extend much further than the pedestrian details of life and work, and she could barely accept a hug or touch of the hand. She acted as if nothing had occurred between them, and maybe she wished that nothing had. Their current life together reminded Ruth of the two women in *The Children's Hour* after the vindictive child's tale had been told — ostracized by the world and not knowing what to say to each other. Until one destroyed herself.

Ruth tapped a pencil on the appointment book, staring out the picture window as if whatever was out there would tell her something different. She should have known. She'd forgotten that she was a stranger in New Bethlehem and nothing could change that. She had allowed herself to believe in something past tomorrow or next week or next year, that the distance was hers — and Belinda's — to travel.

A knock on the front door, which Belinda now kept locked until five minutes before the day's first appointment, almost sent Ruth diving under the desk. A slightly sunburned face, pink behind the straw-colored beard, peered through one of the glass panes in the door.

"Who's there?" Belinda called from the exam room, which she had been straightening for the last half hour.

Ruth was already on her way to the door. "It's Will Polanski," she replied over her shoulder.

"Good morning, Ruth Greene," he said.

She smiled, a trifle grimly, at the bookstore owner. "You do know my name."

"Oh, of course. May I come in?" He wore a plaid cotton shirt whose red stripes only accentuated the fresh ruddiness of his face and well-muscled arms. "Guess who forgot to pack sunscreen when he went to the lake this weekend? But that's not why I'm here."

"Hello. Can I help you?" Belinda stood like a shopkeeper in the waiting area. Her face was drawn, and the well-ironed skirt and blouse seemed to hang from her slender form.

"As a matter of fact, you can. Frank and I caught entirely too many fish on Sunday, and we'd like you two to come over for dinner. If you like fish, that is. If not, we'll go out and reel in a cow or a really choice package of tofu." He smiled. "We thought you might —"

"That's very nice of you," Belinda broke in. "But I am absolutely swamped right now. Maybe another time." She nodded, somewhat stiffly, and excused herself.

Will looked crushed. Before either of them had a chance to react, a young mother came in with three small children who shot like pinballs in three different directions.

"Get back here!" the woman bellowed.

Ruth froze. Will was already backing toward the door.

"I'll be seeing you." He waved. "Let me know if I can do anything," he added, almost in a whisper.

Rain began later in the day, leaving streaks and puddles that looked muddy even when they weren't. At four o'clock, Ruth took her rainbow-striped umbrella and hurried around the corner to *Cover the World*. Will sat behind the counter, and a teenage girl shelved books along a side wall.

"Hi," she said. She could hardly apologize for Belinda giving him the brush-off, but what could she tell him? That Belinda had so blinded herself to the goodwill of others that she probably would have refused a dinner invitation from Jesus Christ himself? "Um, I'm sorry about . . . "

Will looked up from his clipboard. "Coffee?"

The back room looked like someone had dumped the leftover books from every garage sale in the Midwest. Against one cracked wall stood a card table with two folding chairs and a coffee pot whose dribbles had probably not been wiped up in weeks. Will grabbed two matching stoneware mugs from a shelf, filled each with a brew even muddier than Richie's, and set them in the microwave. "It'll be nice and ripe," he assured her with a wink. "So," he said when they sat down. "Any good crap hit your fan lately?"

Ruth took a sip of coffee. "Nothing I shouldn't have expected."

"The expecting's the worst of it." Ruth looked at him quizzically, and he added, "Al spent the better part of two years worrying about what would happen if anyone found out about us, and how he could avoid the least bit of suspicion. He practically built servant's quarters for me out back and said I was his houseboy, bless his skittish little heart."

"Did anyone find out?"

"Not a soul. When he left town, nobody really missed him. Except me." Will tapped at the handle of the mug with his finger. "We didn't have any family here, and certainly no friends — he wasn't about to take that chance. My folks had already told me to take a hike and go to hell, and I didn't have any money left for school, so I stayed here. I've never waved a flag, you understand, but I've never pretended to be anything other than what I am. And sure, there are some people in this town who probably wouldn't set foot in my store and some others I wouldn't want to meet in a dark alley, but don't those folks live in San Francisco too?" He did not wait for her to answer. "Hordes of others know and either don't care or don't care to talk about it. The thing is, I'm theirs. I'm the one they come to when they want a paperback romance, a book that's been out of print since the Stone Age, or an opinion. About anything." He smiled. "My better half, Frank — his ex-wife belongs to a fundamentalist church in Waynesville. They have an eleven-year-old son, and she was going to try to take away Frank's visitation rights. But somehow she never got around to it. More?" He pointed to the pot.

"No, thanks. Haven't you ever thought about leaving here and going someplace friendlier?"

166   NANCY CROWE

"Why would I? I live in a house that's paid for in a blue-collar neighborhood right behind the factory, and the neighbors feed the cat when we're gone and loan me their pickup trucks when I have a load of books to haul. The guy next door has a Confederate flag and a beer gut the size of Alabama, but he'd flatten anyone who came around causing trouble for us. I've got my shop and my Frank and my friends, and I know my way around. I have a piss-poor sense of direction, and I'd get lost anywhere else." Will shrugged, leaned back in his chair, and smiled. "I knew Belinda Boaz was one of the girls."

"I figured you did." Ruth couldn't help smiling, but then she looked at the floor, and at the dust which had already adhered to her shoes. "Maybe if you come by again —"

"You do realize that nobody's upset about her being a dyke, don't you?" Ruth stared at him. "Their knickers are in a twist because she's not the person they thought she was."

"But —"

"Of course she is, in all the ways that matter, but that's not the point. They've got this faceless bigotry and rhetoric on the one hand, and their home-grown girl — the doctor that everyone loves and trusts with their lives — on the other. When you've got so much invested in someone, you don't want them to change. Even if the change is only in what they know, folks around here don't want any part of it."

Ruth sighed. She knew it was pointless, but now it seemed even more so.

"But, you know, it's — well, who let you out early?" Will's face brightened at the middle-aged, balding, pleasant-faced man who had just walked into the back room. "Frank, this is Ruth."

"Hello." He shyly shook her hand.

"I'm going to get these girls over for dinner yet, don't you worry," Will assured him. "Hey, did you remember to pick up some bread?"

He grimaced a little, fidgeting with his tie. "Nope. Forgot. I'll get it after my meeting."

"Well, I'd better go." Ruth stood up. "Thanks…"

"Oh — I was going to say, the funniest thing is when some changes come, people act like it was always that way. Hey, thanks for coming by," Will said. "We'll light a candle and rattle the rosaries for you."

❦

The rain continued into the next day, into an afternoon of sporadic patients and phone calls with tight silences among and between. Ruth leaned her head in her hands, trying to massage the pain from her temples. One of Belinda's regulars, a fifty-something man with allergies to just about everything, watched her from beneath eyebrows that looked like they'd been blow-dried and combed toward his nose. She sat up straight and turned to the computer.

Belinda appeared in the doorway and motioned for him to come in. He stood up in his blue Wiggins Driveshaft jumpsuit and ambled toward her. He paused by the desk and looked at Belinda, then Ruth. "Don't make no difference to me," he grunted, scratching his nose. Belinda gave his shoulder a pat and lightly took his arm as they went into the examination room.

They had been in there no more than three minutes when the front door opened and a wet, wild-eyed Sarah burst in. Dripping and panting, she looked around the waiting room.

"Sarah? What the — stay right there." Ruth grabbed a towel from the supply room and wrapped it around the child. "What on earth are you doing here?"

"I want to see Grandma." She looked around again, as if Ruth were hiding her somewhere.

"Oh, honey." She pulled the towel closer around Sarah. "Do your parents know you're here?"

She shook her head, dark wet strands flipping loose from

the towel. "Mom dropped me off for my piano lesson, and I snuck over here after she drove away. She says I can't see Grandma anymore and she won't tell me why." Tears streamed down Sarah's face.

Ruth's heart sank and took her stomach with it. She gathered the child, wet towel and all, into her arms.

"Why is Mom so mad at Grandma?" She sniffled, and Ruth reached for a box of tissues. "I think she's mad at you, too. Maybe she's really mad at me."

Ruth blinked against her own tears. "Oh, Sarah, it's not your fault. Sometimes… people don't understand each other very well."

"People aren't that hard to understand."

The little girl was right, even if she didn't know exactly what she was saying. "Let's get you into your grandma's office. She's with a patient now, but she should be done pretty soon and you can talk to her."

Ruth situated Sarah in a vinyl chair that wouldn't be adversely affected by a wet child and returned to the reception area. A pregnant woman sat near the door and regarded her with cool suspicion. The moment the jumpsuit-clad patient left, Ruth rushed back to the exam room.

"Sarah's in your office."

"Oh, my God." She dropped a box of tongue depressors onto the counter, and Ruth jumped out of her path.

Through the office doorway, she watched as Belinda wordlessly scooped up her soaking granddaughter and held her on her lap. Ruth returned to her desk and the pregnant woman.

"I'm sorry we're running a little late. Dr. Boaz will be with you in a few minutes."

The woman pushed aside a mop of blonde bangs. "Maybe I oughta leave anyway." She started to ease herself out of the chair.

"No, please don't. She's… an excellent doctor," Ruth said. "She's an excellent person, too."

The woman looked at Ruth, then ran a hand over her rounded belly. "Sure aren't enough of those."

The phone beeped, and Ruth jumped. Belinda never used the intercom.

Belinda closed the office door behind her and met Ruth in the hallway. "I called the piano teacher. She was frantic... thought Sarah had been kidnapped." She brushed at her damp clothes and rubbed her neck. "I also called Eliza, and she's on her way to pick her up."

Ruth sighed. "This doesn't sound good."

"She's mad as hell. Look, why don't you take the car and go home before she gets here? You can pick me up later. I'll call you if I need the car." She pressed her keys into Ruth's hand.

"No."

"Ruth, don't argue with me on this." Her eyes hardened.

She slipped the keys into Belinda's skirt pocket. "I don't want to argue with you, but we're in this together. Remember?"

Belinda let out a long sigh. "Who's next?"

"Carrie Linden. Prenatal. File's in the exam room."

"All right. Let's get her in and I'll deal with Eliza when she gets here. Buzz me, okay?"

Ruth saw Eliza's car pull up outside and had notified Belinda by the time she walked in, face flushed.

"Where's my daughter?" she demanded.

"In the office. Wait," Ruth said as Eliza started back. "Your mom's with a patient, but I think she wants to talk to you."

Eliza paced, drops of water falling from her raincoat. She turned to face Ruth with the stance of a mother bear and the eyes of a wounded cub. "I suppose you still think you're helping."

Ruth swallowed hard and stared at the appointment book, which was full of gaps and crossed-out names, on the desk in front of her.

Belinda appeared a long minute later. "Eliza, Sarah ran over here in the rain because she can't understand why she's not allowed to see her grandmother."

"Well, I'm sure not gonna tell her about... what's been going on. I don't want her learning about that kind of stuff from anyone, especially you." Eliza placed her hands on her hips. "Are you finished?"

"I guess so." Belinda sighed. "I'll get her for you."

"No, I will." Eliza pushed past her mother and stormed down the hall. She led Sarah away like a death row prisoner.

Belinda leaned against the wall and took a few deep breaths, eyes on a chart Ruth knew she wasn't reading. Ruth remembered sitting in a leather chair in the senior pastor's office, then on a bench in the hall while her parents talked with him. The church secretary, who had baked and decorated a big chocolate chip cookie for her when she collected a record amount of canned goods for the youth group's last food drive, barely spoke to her.

Ruth slowly rose from the desk and walked down the hall to where Belinda still leaned against the wall, squinting at the scribbles and printouts like a resident after a double shift. She cleared her throat and tried to keep her voice from breaking. "Is there anything I can do?"

Belinda did not look up from the chart. "No. I have a patient." She strode into the exam room and closed the door behind her.

Chapter Sixteen

Jan resized another block of text and moved a graphic to the other side of her computer screen. "There. How about that?" She peered at the screen, her Peruvian earrings swinging forward.

"It looks good," Ruth said, "but you'd better let me go over the copy again."

"Oh, all right." Jan wrinkled her nose.

They had spent Saturday afternoon, which stretched into evening, working on Foster Advertising's first big account. Jan's cluttered office stood at the top of the stairs in their sixty-year-old yellow house two blocks from the church. It had always been the Presbyterian minister's manse; now it was Jim and Jan's place, decorated with a hodgepodge of rugs from India, tapestries from Guatemala, and a quilt made by the women's guild at Jim's first pastorate. Jim had hurried out around five to meet with a newly-bereaved family. Thirteen-year-old Erica, their only child left at home, was at a friend's house.

Jan sniffed the air. "I bet the lasagna's about ten minutes from being done, so I ought to stick that garlic bread in the oven. Are you ready for a dinner break?"

She certainly was; Belinda had gone to the regional hospital and said she wouldn't be back until late. Ruth dreaded going back to an empty house.

They trooped down the stairs, past the picture window in the front room and into the kitchen, which overlooked the yard next door. The neighbors had been barbecuing out there earlier, and Ruth edged away from the uncovered windows. It wouldn't do any good to be seen in the house alone with the pastor's wife. She was grateful for the gauzy curtains in the breakfast nook, where they sat down to eat.

"Ruth, can I talk you into some more?" Jan's spatula was poised over the pan of vegetarian lasagna.

"No, thanks. It's great, though."

Jan frowned. "Not to sound like your mother or anything, but you've dropped a couple of pounds."

"Maybe so." She wiped her mouth with a napkin.

Jan paused for a moment. "This town — this part of the country, for that matter — never ceases to amaze me," she said. "Has Belinda lost any more patients? Lost them to stupidity, that is."

"A couple more cancelled appointments, with no rescheduling, and we've had some unpleasant phone calls. At home, too," Ruth added.

Jan lightly tapped her fork against the edge of her plate. Several strands of blonde hair had come loose from her ponytail, and she pushed them all back with one hand. "Why don't people just grow up? Back home, this would not be such a brouhaha." She got up to refill Ruth's iced tea. "Jim's been so worried. He wants to help, but he doesn't want to make matters worse for you two in the process."

Ruth nodded. "He came to the office earlier this week."

"So..." Jan sat down again. "Are you coming to church tomorrow?" Before Ruth could get a word out, she held up her hand. "Let me rephrase that. I've been a pastor's wife long enough to know that a personal invitation is what gets people through the door. So will you and Belinda come and sit with Erica and me?"

Ruth tried very hard to swallow the bite of garlic bread she had just taken; she had to wash it down with a gulp of iced tea. Neither she nor Belinda had been to church since Naomi found them together. "Okay," she said finally. "I don't think Belinda will, though."

"Well, tell her she's been personally, specifically invited."

"Will Polanski personally, specifically invited us over for dinner with him and Frank," Ruth said, "and she gave him the brush-off."

"That's too bad. He knows the territory, and they would be a good source of information and support." Jan thought for a moment. "Maybe... well, I guess Belinda's having a tough time."

Ruth nodded. She twisted her paper napkin so hard it tore. "Jan, I need to ask... if you still want me to work for you, with all the talk that's going around. You may have already lost some potential accounts because of me."

Jan finished her water and rattled the ice in the glass. "I'd be lying if I said I didn't have some fears about that."

"I understand." Ruth lowered her eyes. What had her mother said about backing off gracefully? Then again, her mother rarely backed off.

"You also have to understand that one of the reasons I left that agency was the good-old-boy politicking that kept me from giving the best possible service to my clients," she said. "Well, maybe it didn't entirely keep me from doing that, but I wanted to do things my way. Jim would tell you that's nothing new." Jan smiled. "Anyway, if I let a bunch of narrow-minded busybodies stand in the way of working with someone with as much talent and dedication as you, I'm no better than they are, and I shouldn't have my own business."

174   NANCY CROWE

Ruth took a few moments to ponder this. "Thank you," she said softly. "I just hope I'm more of an asset than a liability."

❧

The phone jangled Ruth awake; she had fallen asleep on the living room sofa. Two-thirty-eight, said the clock on the VCR. She listened for a second ring, but heard none and wondered if she dreamed it.

Belinda came down the stairs a minute or two later in her terry-cloth robe, which was so worn it was light enough for summer. "Did the phone wake you?" she asked, as she might a patient.

"It's okay." Ruth rubbed her eyes. "Who was it?"

Belinda shook her head. She walked into the room and stood for a moment or two beside the easy chair next to the sofa, then sat down. "I thought about letting the machine answer, but a lot of my patients won't talk to a machine. Especially at this hour."

Ruth tucked her legs under her. "I suppose not."

When Jim had sat down with Ruth and Belinda — which seemed more like months ago than days — he'd asked what he could do to help. He wanted to address the congregation about what was happening, but would do nothing without their approval. Belinda told him that he might do more harm than good. She related how a few years ago, before Jim came to town, a family at the Lutheran church hosted a Middle Eastern exchange student. Rumors flew that this baby-faced Wiggins accountant and his family were harboring a terrorist, and the threats began. Their well-intentioned pastor preached on nonviolence and held dialogue sessions, inviting all interested parties to air their concerns. The day after one of the dialogues, the church preschool had to be evacuated because of a bomb threat. The student fled in the middle of the night, hitchhiked to Indianapolis, and flew back to his war-torn country where it was safer.

Horrified, Jim asked if he could at least indirectly address the situation in a sermon. Ruth said she would go along with whatever Belinda wanted. After getting him to promise not to use names or specific details, Belinda had reluctantly agreed.

Now she looked at Ruth as if one of them might bolt from the room. At nearly three o'clock on a Sunday morning, what words of God or anyone else — even an invitation to church from the pastor's wife or the perspective of a fellow traveler — would make sense?

"How about some tea?" Ruth asked. Belinda nodded, leaning back in the cushioned recliner.

She wished she could bang pots and pans to drown out whatever ugly words echoed in Belinda's head. She was tempted to phone Naomi at Eunice Christiansen's and see how those gossiping bitches liked being harassed in the middle of the night.

The kettle whistled to a squeal. She returned to the living room with two mugs of chamomile tea, only to find that Belinda had dozed off. Ruth drank her tea and listened to the rhythm of Belinda's breathing until just before dawn, when she quietly stole up to her room.

From the back of the church, Ruth scanned the sanctuary. Naomi sat near the front with Mark, Eliza, and Sarah, and turned around to speak to someone behind her. Ruth drew herself out of view and headed for the ladies' room. No, not a good idea under the circumstances. She waited near the door, pacing and shifting.

There were some genuine hellos from arriving churchgoers, even a hug from the stationery shop owner she'd initially pegged as a good old boy who dressed well. A few people averted their eyes and hurried their families into the sanctuary.

Nancy Crowe

Jan and Erica finally walked up the steps. Erica saw Ruth and smiled, revealing braces with multicolored brackets. "Ruth beat us here, Mom."

The three of them filed into a back pew. "Couldn't get Belinda to come with you?" Jan asked in a low voice.

Ruth shook her head. "She wasn't even up, and I didn't want to wake her." She glanced around and noted a few more raised eyebrows and hardened mouths. It didn't take long before Naomi saw her, too; she quickly turned away and leaned across Mark to whisper to Eliza.

Ruth winced when she heard the Old Testament reading on the Ten Commandments: you shall not, you shall not. She fought to squelch the silent shouts that she had been set up, that this pack of Christians was no different from any other. Jim and Jan were real; they were friends who just happened to be Christians. She forced herself to breathe slowly and listen.

"We hear a lot about the Ten Commandments today," Jim said, "especially when someone wants to post them in a public place. I don't know what Jesus would say about that. He did say: Look, folks, it's not that hard. All you really have to remember is to love God and love your neighbor. The rest will more or less take care of itself, if you let it.

"Are we doing that here?" He took off his glasses. "Or are we so caught up in declaring what's right and what's wrong that we have no energy left for loving one another? Now, by that I don't mean the 'love the sinner, hate the sin' thing. People say that without thinking about how disrespectful and un-loving it is, and I don't believe anyone buys it."

The quiet was broken only by muffled throat-clearing and shifting in the pews. Ruth did not dare turn her head.

"According to the text, God gave the people this message through Moses: You shall love the stranger, for you were strangers yourselves and you know what it's like. Many years later, Jesus said not only to love God and neighbor, but that when we welcome a stranger we welcome Jesus himself. Not one word is said in either case about how the stranger looks, what the stranger believes, or who the stranger loves." He wiped his forehead. "Friends, when we oppress the stranger, sooner or later that stranger will be us."

When he had finished speaking, he sat down and buried his nose in the bulletin and hymnal in his lap. Ruth saw him glance up only once or twice during the offertory.

Jim shook her hand after the service, then held it as if he were taking her pulse. "You don't look so good," he said quietly. "Can you hang around for a minute?"

Jim's study was a small but airy room filled with books and more items from his travels. He closed the door, hung up his heavy black robe, and turned to Ruth, who was finding it next to impossible to keep the tears back. He put both arms around her, and she gave up and sobbed against his shoulder.

"Oh, my," he said after the sobs had subsided. "They warned us about this in seminary, but something told me I was safe with you." He hugged her tightly before letting her go.

Ruth met his mischievous gaze and could not help smiling. They sat down and she took the box of tissues he offered. "That was a great sermon." She blotted her eyes and cheeks.

"Thanks. I hoped you and Belinda would both be here this morning."

"I did, too." Ruth leaned forward, face in her hands. "I love her more than I thought I could love anyone. That's why I can't stand causing her all this pain."

He frowned. "What makes you think it's you who's causing the pain?"

"I'm the stranger here! I'm that damn lesbian from San Francisco who corrupted one member of the family out there, and then came here and corrupted another one. If it wasn't for me, everything would be fine."

"If it wasn't for Jesus, we'd all be fine. Right?"

"Huh?"

"Jesus was a stranger just about everywhere he went, and his home town didn't exactly take a shine to him, either. But he was love personified."

Ruth hesitated. "Are you comparing me to Jesus?"

"Sure, why not?"

"Because he was… he's God. Or has something changed since I was in Sunday school?"

"That was a course in Christology I didn't get to take. And don't tell the elders, but I think we get way too hung up on that."

Ruth shook her head. "All right, Jim, you've lost me."

"Work with me here. Jesus embodied love, and that certainly came from God. Whether he was *the* Son of God or not — in the final analysis, I don't think that's nearly as important as what he did with the divine compassion, courage, and insight that God gave him. Problem was, people then and now don't appreciate love in all its manifestations. We're afraid of it, so we get out the crosses and nails. We all do it, in one way or another." He adjusted his glasses. "Is any of this making sense?"

"I suppose." Ruth's gaze wandered from an embroidered Twenty-third Psalm on the wall to an African figure carved of smooth, dark wood, arms outstretched, on the credenza. "But it doesn't tell me what I should do."

"Of course not. It's never that easy." Jim sighed and leaned back in his chair. "What you do, or think, is strictly up to you. Personally, I believe that Christians have karma. The Hindus and Buddhists didn't corner the market on that one. Jesus even said that your treasure will be found where your heart is. Or is that the other way around?" He looked around for a Bible, then waved his hand. "Same either way. There are exceptions to this, like anything else, but if you concentrate on the crosses and nails, that's what your treasure is likely to be. And that's not a treasure I'd care to find. Besides, the cross-and-nail thing has been done."

❧

Ruth closed the heavy church door and stood on the step, letting her eyes adjust to the midday sun. Belinda was probably up; she may have even fixed lunch. Maybe they could have a nice, relaxed meal and talk.

She walked around the corner to where she had parked Belinda's car in back of the church.

"Where you goin', bulldyke?"

Three young men, maybe in their late teens, appeared from a doorway and blocked her path. Ruth recognized two of them from church. Brian. The blonde one's name was Brian. She'd met him at the picnic, and he was related to someone who went to school with Naomi.

She edged away from them. "Brian, what —"

"Shut up!" The biggest of the three wore a dark stubble of hair and a T-shirt from some rock concert or other. Ruth smelled smoke and sweat as he loomed closer, the other two behind him. "Go back with all those other queers."

Ruth moved toward the curb. One of the others, a short, muscular type with painful-looking acne, stepped in front of her. "You'll get the hell out of here if you know what's good for you," he said.

This was where it would end. They were going to kill her, and then they would go after Belinda, and the world would be through with both of them. But the young men, really blown-up boys, just stared at her with narrowed eyes.

Slowly, she walked around and away from them. The three watched like wolves as she got into her car. She would stay calm. She would get away. She locked the door, started the engine and glanced in the rear-view mirror. One of them — no, two — got into an old yellow sedan with duct tape holding the headlights in place.

God, no. Heart pounding, she took off down Main Street.

Ruth drove up one street and down another, scanning the rearview mirror every two seconds. The damn town wasn't large enough for her to lose them, but she could not risk being run off some back country road.

Martin Street? No, it was one-way north. Spring Avenue? It led to a dead end or cul-de-sac. Or did it? She screeched around the corner.

She checked the rearview mirror again. A silver minivan was about half a block behind her. What was behind the minivan? Something yellow?

Her eyes snapped back to the road just in time to see a little boy, no more than six or seven, on his bicycle and directly in her path. She swerved and barely missed the child. He pedaled furiously away, wailing.

She could have killed him. A drop of perspiration rolled down her side.

She drove around a corner and back onto a main road. They had to be right behind her, just out of view. If you think you're being followed, don't drive home, the officer had told the women in her college dormitory. Go to a police station or a well-lighted, well-populated business. The police station had to be somewhere near the courthouse. She drove around the square but did not see it. Bad idea anyway. Some redneck cop would laugh in her face.

On a Sunday in Indiana, few New Bethlehem businesses were open except a couple of restaurants and a gas station. Restaurants were no good. Full of church people at this hour.

Ruth pulled into the gas station, in front of a dingy little building that pretended to be a convenience store, and tried to collect herself. Out of the corner of her eye, she saw a man approach the car from behind. Shit, what a mistake. She threw the car into drive and took off, tires squealing.

After half an hour of driving around town, she felt reason-

ably sure that no one was following her and took a long, cir-
cuitous route back to Belinda's house.

ᕮᕳ

Belinda was stirring something in a large metal bowl when
Ruth burst through the door, and she nearly dropped the spoon.
"What's wrong?" She fetched a glass of water and made Ruth
sit down.

Fear stared back at Ruth as she recounted the incident.
She flinched, and despised herself for it, when Belinda reached
to comfort her. Belinda moved away and sat across the table
with her hands folded, eliciting the facts.

"The guy at the gas station was Joey," she said finally,
"and it's the county's last surviving full-service station. He's
been working there for years and would chase off or throttle
anyone who behaved in a threatening way." She got up, refilled Ruth's glass, and filled one for herself. "I think I know
who two of the boys were. One was a patient when he was a
little kid. The parents seemed nice enough, brought him in
when they were supposed to and paid their bills on time. He
cried when I gave him shots, but somewhere between then
and now he turned into a goddamn thug who could accost a
woman not two-thirds his size." Both her hands gripped the
edge of the sink.

Ruth quietly got up from her chair and stood just a few
inches behind Belinda, her fingers barely brushing Belinda's
sleeves.

"Why don't you go upstairs and rest?"

Ruth's arms, still trembling, fell to her sides.

ᕮᕳ

Although Belinda encouraged her to take the day off, Ruth
insisted on going to work Monday morning. They had gone to
the police station Sunday evening and the officer took a re-

port, seldom looking up from his notepad. Belinda gave him the names and addresses of Brian and the other boy from the church directory, and Ruth's description of the third seemed familiar to the young policeman. He said he'd be in touch.

"Oh, no," Belinda said almost as soon as she parked the car in front of her office.

Whatever had been thrown through the front picture window had left a wide, jagged hole surrounded by an intricate network of cracks. Ruth sprang from the car; Belinda was already halfway to the door. A brick lay surrounded by glittering shards and slivers of glass on the waiting room floor.

"Don't touch it," Belinda ordered, stepping around the glass to get to the phone, "until I call the police. Again."

Ruth stormed from room to room, throwing closet doors open and looking behind chairs and under desks. God help anyone who might be lurking in this place of healing. She returned to the waiting room to see Belinda crouched on the floor, lifting the brick with one hand.

"Belinda, put that down!" The force in her voice surprised her. It surprised Belinda, too, and she let the brick fall to the floor. "Did you call?"

"I'm about to." She stood and tiptoed away from the breakage.

Belinda must have been looking for a note attached to the brick, some confirmation that this was not a random act. But Ruth needed no note to tell her who the target was, or why the brick had come crashing in. She hesitated for about ten seconds before following Belinda back to the office, only to find the door closed.

Chapter Seventeen

Naomi left Richie's and walked down Main Street in the midday sun, rummaging in her purse for her sunglasses. The Christian book and church supply store had been in the old Forrester building since Marina and Cara were little. The couple who ran it drew a steady business from most of the churches in the region and the hungry readers who came in looking for advice on parenting, personal finance, or getting through heartache from a Christian point of view. Marina had bought quite a few books there with her babysitting money — biographies, Bible studies, inspiration for Christian athletes, strategies for becoming a godly woman. For years it had been the only bookstore in town, but now there was a used bookstore just around the corner from Belinda's office, run by that nice young man who sometimes came to Richie's for take-out and always had a friendly word or two for the girls.

For this, however, the Christian store was the best bet. She gave up on finding the sunglasses and stood on the corner, blinking in the sun. Was it on Ryan Street, or Maple? There was the paint store, and Buddy Gribben's insurance office, and the bookstore was just a block over. But which way? She looked from one end of the block to the other. Cars glided through the intersection without slowing to negotiate the terrain, foreign models and minivans that would never have been seen here ten years ago unless they were from out of town. Unlike San Francisco, this place was as level as a football field; you could see what was over the next hill because there was no next hill. Just that morning, when she parked on Main Street, she'd curbed her wheels out of habit.

Ten years was not such a long time when you'd lived for almost seventy, and yet nothing about New Bethlehem truly looked the same after those ten years in San Francisco. When she drove up one street and down another, she saw most of the same front porches and storefronts and signs she'd seen every day before Ed hauled them west. A lot of the same folks were still around, grayer like she was, but new ones had arrived and acted like they'd always been here. There was a different air about the town, a sense that the dinginess of the recession had been painted over before it was cleaned up.

Naomi caught a glimpse of her reflection in a store window. Other people's mental pictures of Naomi, and the husband and daughters she left with, were probably just as blurry and faded as hers.

She turned down Maple and there it was. The praying hands sign was still on the door, and Southern gospel still played on the stereo speakers inside. A tall woman, probably athletic like Marina, paid for a stack of books with a credit card. When she turned around, Naomi saw that she wore a clerical collar. Well, that was a first for New Bethlehem, unless she was just passing through. The woman thanked the clerk and picked up the bag like it weighed nothing at all. "Good morning," she said to Naomi.

"Morning." Naomi looked after her, then at the floppy-haired young man behind the counter, whom she did not recognize. He could be the owner's son, nephew, or anyone.

She wandered down one of the side aisles. New Bethlehem Presbyterian had allowed women to be deacons and elders since the sixties or seventies, but Naomi had never done either one. The Lord chose only men to help him spread the word, and she supposed he knew what he was doing. She'd gone to her church in San Francisco, which had no denomination telling them what to do, for two years before she even noticed that all the pastors and leaders were men, and that was fine by her. The first few times she led the Wednesday night women's prayer and praise meeting, she'd about broken out in hives. One of the ladies assured her it was all right because it was a women's service. The Apostle Paul had said a woman should not teach or have authority over a man, so Naomi was in the clear. Besides, her friend added with a wink, no man was brave enough to be in the presence of the Spirit when the women got going.

Naomi turned down another aisle and fished a folded-up piece of paper out of her purse. A woman at church had told her about a book by a doctor who'd helped many homosexuals leave that lifestyle. It was a sickness that could be healed with proper treatment and faith, and some places even had groups for them like they did for drunks and drug addicts. If the store didn't have the book, she'd have them order it by express mail. Surely Belinda would heed the words of a doctor like herself. Obviously, she was lonely and needed help.

Naomi still took Sarah to her lessons and other activities, but the child hardly spoke anymore. The other day she'd gotten into a fight at day camp, a knock-down drag-out that left the other girl with a bruise over her left eye. "She just made me mad," Sarah said.

Eliza didn't know what to do with her, either. They explained to Sarah that her grandmother was having some problems, and that's why she couldn't see her. When the child asked about Ruth, Naomi said Ruth had done bad things and Sarah mustn't go near her.

Naomi ordered the book, bought a colorful picture book about Noah and the animals for Sarah, and headed back around the corner and down Main. She had half an hour before she was supposed to go over and help Lula at the day care. Eunice was going to join them, too.

Eunice had been quite gracious in letting Naomi stay in her guest room and share meals on her screened-in porch with the glass table and bamboo chairs. But it was time to get her own place and have what was left in San Francisco shipped to New Bethlehem.

She paused outside McKay Real Estate. An agent there, whose name she'd long since forgotten, had helped her and Ed buy their first house. She knew no one who worked there now, but it might be a good place to ask about affordable places to rent, maybe even buy.

On the other side of the street, Ruth stopped outside the tiny American Automobile Association office. For a minute or two she just stood there as if she were either window-shopping or lost, and then she went inside. Naomi vaguely recalled Ruth wanting a map of the area when they first came to town, and she'd asked about places to go hiking. That must be what she was after.

The sight of Ruth, bare-shouldered in Belinda's bed, was still etched in her mind. That girl had no trouble finding anything.

❧

"Whaddya think?" Greta held a form-fitting summer dress with spaghetti straps in front of her.

Naomi turned from the clearance rack. "Go for it."

"Maybe forty years ago, but not now." Greta laughed and put the dress back.

"Will you look at this." Naomi held out the sleeve of a dress with a price tag on it. "This is an outlet mall, for heaven's sakes. Aren't they supposed to be cheaper?"

"You'd think," Greta said.

The two of them hadn't talked since Naomi left Greta's

house, the day after she left Belinda's. She really didn't hold it against Greta; Irvin Robinson was an old cuss fifty years ago, and now he was just an older cuss. Then Greta had called her at Eunice's and asked if she wanted to go shopping. Eunice was out having her hair done, so Naomi didn't have to invite her. She'd picked Greta up on the way out of town and they'd gabbed just like always.

The outlet mall, forty miles away, had only been a gleam in a developer's eye when Naomi moved to San Francisco. Sprawling and still smelling like sawdust and fresh paint, it was the perfect place to refresh her black-belt bargain hunting skills and not be jostled by people speaking everything but English.

"I'm ready to sit down for a bit," Naomi said. "This knee of mine doesn't allow for marathon shopping."

"Honey, my knees gave out so long ago I don't even pay attention anymore," Greta said, "but that's a good idea."

They settled on a bench in the courtyard, out of the sun. Teenage girls in low-riding jeans and too much lipstick sauntered up and down the walks, and mothers herded children from store to store in search of clothes and shoes for school. You never knew what the kids were going to want or what it would cost, and they'd outgrow it all by spring. That was one aspect of raising her girls that Naomi didn't miss in the least.

"Do you know what happened to Ruth?" she asked Greta. "I heard about some boys bothering her over by the church."

Greta arranged the bags under the bench. "Apparently there were three, and two of them were Brian Philpot and Sean Stambaugh. I don't know who the other one was, and it's all second- and third-hand information anyhow."

"Wilma Philpot's grandson?"

Greta nodded. "Sean's been coming to youth group with Brian for a while now, and his parents joined the church last spring." She shook her head. "I can't imagine anyone — from our church, especially — doing such a thing."

188   NANCY CROWE

"Why would… when did this happen?"

"Sunday, not too long after church let out." Greta sighed. "I suppose you also heard about Belinda's office window getting broken."

"They think the kids did that, too?"

"Who knows." Greta examined the nails on her long, slender fingers, and then rested both hands in her lap. "Naomi, did you ever think that talking about Ruth and Belinda the way you've done might cause a whole world of trouble?"

Naomi drew back. "Are you saying I'm to blame for this?"

"The people who harassed Ruth and broke the window are responsible for what they did. But honey, there's a lot of talk and a lot of hurt going around. I'm sorry, but I do think you had a part in that. A big part." Greta turned to face her friend.

"But… it's not right, and…" Naomi spluttered. "Them two are the ones doing wrong, not me."

"Well, who appointed you to be the messenger? Naomi, you know very well how things get around town and get twisted every step of the way. Those women have done a lot to help you, and no matter what you thought about them, didn't you have the sense to know your tongue might make matters worse for everyone?" Greta's face was red.

Naomi could not remember a time when Greta had been more angry, or when she had been angry at all. She tried to think of a suitable response while Greta caught her breath. "They brought it on themselves."

"It was none of your damn business."

Naomi flinched. Greta had not said so much as shucky-darn since high school. "Belinda's my cousin. Shouldn't I look out for her?"

"Oh, for heaven's sakes, Naomi, Belinda is a grown woman. A doctor. She's got to be the smartest person in town."

"I oughta be shot for lettin' that girl come out here with me." Naomi leaned forward, head in her hands.

Greta put a hand on Naomi's shoulder. "Don't you think it's time to quit blaming and figure out how to clean up this mess?"

"Greta, it's just not right." Naomi would not look at her. "You know that."

Greta said nothing for a few moments. "I asked Jim Foster a while back about all those Bible passages that people cite. I don't remember much of what he said, and I didn't understand it all anyway. But it sounds like there's been a lot of wrong interpretation over the years. I've read articles where scientists and counselors say some folks are born that way."

Naomi snorted. "What do they know?"

"Just as much as you or I." She stretched her legs out in front of her.

Naomi watched a young mother bargain with her two little girls; if they would go into just a couple more stores with her, they could each have an ice cream cone. "Was Ruth hurt?" she asked.

"I don't think so. Not on the outside, anyway."

Neither of them said much on the drive back to New Bethlehem. Naomi dropped Greta off and drove back through town, slowing the car in front of Belinda's office. The sharp-edged hole in the window had been covered with plastic and duct tape. It was like trying to tape someone's mouth shut after they'd already spoken.

　　　　　　　　　　　　NANCY CROWE

Chapter Eighteen

The doorbell rang just after eight, and both of them jumped.

Ruth looked out the window. Lula stood on the front step in one of her appliqued T-shirts, this one with a smiling tiger, holding a foil-wrapped object which was too big to be a brick.

"Lula," Ruth whispered. Belinda, stationed at the dining room table with several insurance forms, turned her pen around and around in one hand and then nodded. Ruth swallowed hard and opened the door.

"Good evening," Lula said. "Is Belinda home?"

Ruth stepped aside, wondering how soon she would regret letting Lula in. "She's in the dining room."

Lula entered, holding the foil-wrapped object aloft. "I come bearing chocolate zucchini cake," she said to Belinda, "in the hopes that you'll check my blood pressure real quick. You told me at my last physical to watch it, but I just haven't had the time to come by the office."

Belinda took off her glasses. "And you know very well I can't resist your chocolate zucchini cake. Have a seat in the kitchen and I'll be right with you."

Lula sat at the table and neatly crossed her legs as if she

had come to tea. Ruth silently went back to putting away the dishes; even weather talk might be more than she could handle.

Belinda returned with the stethoscope and blood pressure cuff she kept in the linen closet and wrapped the cuff around Lula's right arm. She tightened the cuff, released it, listened, and watched the gauge. "It's a hair on the high side... but I think you're doing fine, all things considered." She removed the cuff with a raspy ripping sound.

Lula patted her sleeve back into place. "You find out who broke your window?"

Belinda set the equipment on the table. "The police are looking into it."

"Makes no sense." Lula looked from one to the other, then stood up. "Well, I'll let you get back to your evening. Thank you, Belinda."

"Thank you for the cake," Belinda said quietly.

"You all need anything, just knock on my door, you hear?"

Ruth glanced up and realized Lula was speaking to her, too. She nodded and tried to look gracious.

"Sure," Belinda said, not looking at either of them.

Lula stood up straight, a duchess even in a T-shirt with a tiny smear of chocolate on the front. "Belinda Boaz, I know who my friends are. I hope you do, too."

After several days, the police had no suspects in the window-breaking. Ruth wondered how hard they were looking. She went to see an attorney whose mother was one of Belinda's patients, and he advised her that taking further legal action against the boys was not likely to bear fruit. Deflated, she drove back to Belinda's office. It was two blocks away, but she felt safer in a locked car.

"There has to be something someone can do," she told Belinda after dinner. "They shouldn't be able to just do what they did and not face any consequences."

"I agree." Belinda dusted the mantel for the second time in a week.

"What about your window? Don't you want some kind of justice for that?"

She picked up two photos with one hand, swept the rag over the surface beneath them, and set them down. "Of course. But I'm not likely to ever know who did it. It may be the same kids, and it may not be."

Ruth opened her mouth to argue, but decided against it. This conversation was too important for her to put Belinda on the defensive. She waited for her to finish dusting and sit down. "You must be very frustrated."

Belinda leaned an elbow on the arm of the sofa. "Sure I am, but what good does that do? I have to concentrate on what's left... the patients who haven't bailed out on me, for one thing."

"I'm here, too," Ruth said.

Belinda rearranged some magazines and journals on the coffee table. "You're here, and you're treated like a leper. You're afraid to go out or answer the phone."

Ruth took a deep breath. "Come to San Francisco with me. Gay doctors are no big deal there."

"Ruth, I can't do that. I have a practice I've worked for years to build, and I have a daughter who might, if I'm lucky, start speaking to me again sometime before I die. This is my home. I can't just leave."

"But — when we talked about that earlier, you said... that is, you seemed to think it was a possibility," Ruth countered.

"Well, I was wrong." Belinda looked away.

Ruth leaned forward in her chair. "Belinda, I want to be with you. I want you to be with me, too. But it's like part of you either died or just went away." She blinked hard. Not now. "I know I brought this on, and I don't want to—"

"No." Belinda put down a stack of journals. "It is not your fault."

"None of this would have happened if I hadn't come here, or at least if I'd kept my feelings to myself." Ruth was crying, despite her best efforts not to. "You hardly even talk to me anymore."

"What the hell do you want from me?" Belinda snapped. "You expect me to make small talk and entertain you while my career and family fall apart? You want to pin another set of expectations on me, just so you can be disappointed too? Is that what you want?" Her voice had risen to a tone Ruth had never heard before.

She stared at Belinda's reddened face. "No," she said quietly, "but you could let me be there for you."

Belinda looked her in the eyes. "I can't."

Her words struck Ruth in the solar plexus. "Why?" Belinda did not answer.

Ruth tried to get her breath back. "I feel like I might as well not be here at all."

Belinda put her face in her hands, rubbing her eyes. "Then why don't you just go back to San Francisco?"

"Fine, I will." Ruth stood up. "I've already bought a ticket."

Belinda looked up, the color leaving her face. "What?"

"When that brick came through the window, I knew who it was for." She left the room. Belinda would see no more tears.

"Ruth!"

She paused halfway up the stairs, wanting more than anything to turn and walk back down.

"When did you buy a ticket?" Belinda approached the foot of the stairs.

Ruth's heart jumped into her throat. "It doesn't matter now, does it? You got what you wanted." She walked the rest of the way upstairs, closed the door of the catch-all room, and started packing.

Chapter Nineteen

The cab driver, a young Hispanic man with a shy smile, helped Ruth carry her bags up to the apartment. With her last days in Indiana still hanging over her like a toxic cloud, she almost asked him to stay while she checked each room and closet.

After sending him off with fare and tip, she locked the front door and opened the patio door and a few windows. The place smelled musty after being closed up all summer, and yet a trace of Marina's perfume remained. She had moved around what furniture she could — hers, plus the items neither Marina nor Naomi wanted — spreading it out to make the apartment look less empty. It hadn't worked. Each item stood apart from the next like strangers at a bus station.

The answering machine in the bedroom blinked furiously, having reached its capacity. She sat down with pen and paper and played back the tape. There were messages from friends, wondering where Ruth was, and one or two for Marina from people who didn't know she'd moved away.

There were also a few from Ruth's mother. Ruth had left a message on her parents' machine before she and Naomi departed for Indiana, letting them know she was driving to Indiana with Marina's mother and didn't know when she'd be back. She had given them Belinda's phone number so they could reach her in case of an emergency.

The first message was bright and curious: "Hi, honey, are you back from your trip? Give us a call. Bye." Then: "Ruth, are you there? Call us back." On the third message her mother's voice tightened ever so slightly, the way it used to when Ruth wasn't in trouble but might soon be: "You must still be in Indiana... I guess I'll call the number you left in your message... damn, where did I write that down... anyway, I guess I'll talk to you later."

Ruth pressed the stop button. What was going on? Her mother had not called Belinda's house, or at least not left a message. Maybe Ruth had left the wrong number — or Naomi had given Ruth the wrong number. She decided to listen to the rest of the tape before she panicked.

A few messages later: "Got your postcard. I didn't know Indiana was that pretty. When you get back, give us a call. We love you. Bye."

There was even one from her father: "Hi, kiddo, just wanted to say hello... so, hi, I guess. Bye."

Ruth smiled. Her father, so articulate in the classroom, turned into a tongue-tied adolescent on answering machines. She picked up the phone.

"Hey, Mom."

"Well, it's about time. Did Marina's mom get settled all right?"

"I think so." Ruth was glad this was not a face-to-face conversation.

"That's good. It was so nice of you to go out there, and then to stay and work for that doctor all summer. You're a regular Girl Scout."

"Yeah, that's me. How's Dad?"

"He's got his nose buried in about six textbooks, getting the syllabi ready."

"I've got to do that too." She hesitated. "Did you try to call me in Indiana? What was —"

"Oh... no. By the time I dug the number out from under all the other debris in this kitchen, I decided to just wait until you got back." Ruth heard her mother put something down or shift the phone from one ear to the other. "Did Marina fly out to Indiana? You didn't say she was going with you on the road trip."

"No, she moved out a few months ago. She's in Seattle."

Her mother fell silent for a few seconds. "I'm sorry."

"Thanks." Ruth did not know what else to say.

"And you still went all the way out there with — what's her name?"

"Naomi."

"Right. My goodness. Well. Listen, things are crazy right now, but you'll have to come for dinner soon."

"Sounds good." After she hung up, she tried to remember the last time she had seen her parents.

She stretched out on the queen-size bed, looking sideways at the clock. It was already ten in Indiana, and she tried not to think of Belinda at home alone. Belinda may have taken some small measure of comfort from having another human being in the house, but she was better off with Ruth far away.

"Will you... let me know how you are?" Belinda had asked that morning before she left for work.

Was that all? "Sure."

Belinda had shouldered her briefcase and turned to leave. Ruth gently took hold of the strap and pulled Belinda into her arms, briefcase and all, knowing she might be pushed away, knowing she already had been.

"Goodbye, Ruth." Belinda hesitated, then kissed her on the cheek.

She couldn't go. She wouldn't. But she had to. Jan would be there in a few minutes to take her to the nearest commuter airport, where a prop plane and then two different jets would take her past the point of turning back.

"Take care," Ruth said. Don't go. Don't let me go.

"You, too. God bless." Belinda had realigned her briefcase and hurried out.

Ruth stretched out on the bed, the weight of the trip settling over her. It had taken so long to get to New Bethlehem, and in only a few hours she was back. Maybe, now that she was back in her place, God would bless.

Chapter Twenty

Naomi closed the window of her small apartment. Her bones hadn't weathered an Indiana winter in ten years, and the chill in the autumn air caught her off guard. Everything would get grayer — the sky, the snow along the curb, the coats people wore. Even when the sun was out, the world seemed ready to forget everything and fold up.

The letter still sat on the coffee table the moving van had brought from San Francisco with the rest of her things in September. Naomi sat down, wrapped herself in one of the handmade afghans she had draped over the couch, and read it again.

Marina must have called Lucia, Naomi's only trusted neighbor on Estancia Boulevard, and been given Belinda's address. Belinda had crossed out her address, written in Naomi's new one, and put the small envelope back in the mail. Had Marina worried when she couldn't reach her mother? Had she paced up and down in the apartment Naomi had never seen, in a city Naomi had never visited, and wondered where her mother was?

Marina's job was going well and she liked Seattle. She asked about Naomi's plans for Thanksgiving and Christmas;

would she be coming back to San Francisco? Marina closed the brief letter by saying she hoped her mother was well.

Naomi stuffed the letter back into the envelope, which bore no return address. There was no mention of the phony post office box number Marina had given her mother months ago, from which all letters had bounced back unopened. Not a word about any hurt feelings, and no indication that Marina was willing to travel the distance to see her mother anytime soon. Naomi knew she was lucky to hear from Marina at all.

Hell, she was lucky to know where she was herself. It used to be she could look around at any crowd in New Bethlehem, in church, at a festival in the park, or in a restaurant, and recognize almost every face. Now she knew about half, at best, and at her age you could never tell when memory might mistakenly fill in a blank — or leave one.

She still went to her women's circle at church and sometimes watched Sarah after school. She even drove over to the hospital a couple of times with Lula, who had started volunteering there once or twice a month. Lula didn't want to go by herself on the day she knew she'd be visiting an AIDS patient, so she asked Naomi to come along.

"Why me?" Naomi had asked, fastening the seatbelt in Lula's chocolate-colored Lincoln.

Lula adjusted her sunglasses and backed out of the driveway. "Well, what other pressing engagements do you have today?"

Naomi shrugged and looked out the window. There was no saying no to Lula once she'd made up her mind that you were going to be part of one of her projects, and it was actually quite a compliment when she did.

She had hovered near the door while Lula sat beside the young man's bed. He couldn't have been any older than Marina, but he looked like the pictures she'd seen of people in concentration camps; his eyes were lost in his head. His face

NANCY CROWE

showed a little more life as he and Lula talked; Naomi couldn't hear what they were saying. The nurse had whispered that no one had come to see him in at least a week. He had once been a tiny baby boy like Evan with the whole world in front of him; someone must have cared, sometime.

I'm not letting you go through this by yourself, Ruth had shouted by the side of the road as cars, semis, and the rest of the world whipped past them. It was too big a promise for anyone in their right mind to make.

Eliza had invited Naomi for Thanksgiving and she accepted, wondering if Belinda would be there. Eliza was speaking to her mother again, but not much.

Eliza had told her father the whole story about Belinda and Ruth, expecting him to be just as devastated as she was, but he'd known about Belinda since right around the time they got divorced. He told Eliza it had bothered him at first, but then it made him feel better in an odd sort of way — that the problems they had weren't so much because he messed up or Belinda did. It was just the way things were, and he knew something was up between her and Ruth when he came over for dinner with Eliza. Naomi replayed the bits and pieces she could recall of that evening; what had Griff seen in those few hours that she'd missed all summer?

Eliza, looking the way Marina and Cara used to when they didn't quite have their algebra figured out, had relayed this conversation to Mark and Naomi as she cooked spaghetti for Sarah's birthday dinner.

"I always knew your folks had good common sense," Mark had said, slipping an arm around his wife and looking at her tenderly. "And good uncommon sense."

Naomi wondered how any man in Griff's position wouldn't be humiliated and outraged, and have nothing further to do with the mother of his child. But there they sat at Richie's last week, chatting over sandwiches and fries while the girls from the high school volleyball team giggled and called to each other, ponytails flipping, at several tables along the wall. Naomi almost didn't hear the cashier ring up her takeout pastrami sandwich. Belinda and Griff had been friends for most of their lives, and maybe something like that couldn't help but last. The best friendships always did, somehow.

Apparently family was something else again. After several weeks away from church, Belinda showed up one Sunday and even stayed for coffee. Naomi went up and asked how she was.

"Naomi, I don't want to talk to you," Belinda said, her face stone-cold, "until you learn how to think before you speak."

She had left Naomi standing alone by the painting her uncle had willed to the church, of the young Jesus in the temple. A few people had been watching out of the corners of their eyes while they pretended to stand around drinking coffee and talking about the weather or how they were going to replace the wheezy old pipe organ, but they looked away. Naomi felt her cheeks flame up like hot coals. She'd thought before she spoke to Belinda that morning after weeks of not speaking to her, and this was how Belinda acted — snubbing her in front of all these people.

Greta had been nowhere in sight; Irvin wasn't even parked in his usual chair by the door. Naomi did not see much of her these days, but she knew Greta had been spending some time with Belinda. That was probably all right; Belinda needed a good influence in her life.

Naomi had driven to the library two towns over and looked at just about every book they had on homosexuality. There were books written by doctors, scholars, homosexuals, preachers, even homosexual preachers. Everyone had done tons of research on the Bible and come up with all these different answers. What was anybody supposed to believe?

Naomi drew the afghan tighter around her. She knew she didn't understand any of it. She didn't understand Marina,

Belinda, or Ruth for that matter. Considering that two of them weren't speaking to her and one had only written to her after six months of silence, maybe it didn't matter anyway.

Chapter Twenty-One

Fortunately, the English department chair was able to give Ruth her job back. Since the class schedule had already been reshuffled, she ended up teaching two remedial composition sections that no one else wanted along with the regular class she had taught many times before. New faces filled her classroom, and every week she brought home stacks of papers to fill her mind, crowding out anything else. Marina had left some advance rent money, and Ruth put off looking for a smaller place or trying to make her current abode look less vacated.

Willa Cather had only been able to put the Midwest into perspective after she escaped it. San Francisco's streets, stores, and restaurants vibrated with color, its young and not-so-young denizens with piercings and hair of every shade and style. Hills and mountains lifted the ground and everything on it into the sky. How could Ruth have wanted to live in a place so flat and unyielding? She walked through the Castro and listened to the hum of energy she had never heard before. Perspective would come later, if at all. It made sense to be here.

Except when she was alone, or when she tried to tell her

NANCY CROWE

friends where she'd been all summer. One said Ruth was lucky not to have been killed out there in the Bible Belt. Another said she was fortunate to be free of anyone even remotely associated with Marina or her mother. Yet another said that Ruth must have some unresolved issues and that Belinda had used her. But she hadn't, of course; Belinda had gained nothing from Ruth.

❧

The light blue envelope had a return address label with a tiny gardening spade and "I.S. Robinson" over the address in script. Ruth dropped the other mail and a tote bag full of papers onto the kitchen table and ripped open the envelope.

> *Dear Ruth,*
>
> *Well, I guess I'm being sneaky today. I copied your address out of Belinda's big calendar and address book while she was in the powder room! I don't know why I sneaked. I just wanted to let you know how much we miss you here in New Bethlehem.*
>
> *Naomi is OK, I guess. Kind of quiet lately (and you know how unusual that is). Belinda is doing OK, but I know she misses you. Her practice is getting back on its feet. I think all the fuss has mostly blown over.*
>
> *My younger sister Ruby died a few years ago, and she left everything to the lady she'd shared a house with for over 20 years. The family didn't ever talk about it, but I practically raised my baby sister and I keep feeling like I missed something. Talking to Belinda sure does help.*
>
> *Irvin is taking me out to dinner tonight, so I'd best close. Are you coming back soon?*
> *Love,*
> *Greta*

Ruth reread Greta's even script several times before she

had to put the letter down. Greta and Naomi had been friends for well over half a century; if anyone could see the good in Naomi, it was Greta. If anyone could see hope anywhere, it was Greta.

✎෨

Ruth's mother set a glass dish full of twice-baked potatoes, seasoned with Worcestershire sauce and chopped onion, on the table.

"We haven't had these in years," Ruth said.

"Hey, if you can't have this stuff at Thanksgiving, when can you?" her mother said over her shoulder, already on her way back into the kitchen.

"What else do we need?" Ruth followed her.

Ruth's father hovered between kitchen and dining room as first his wife, then his daughter zipped past him. "Are you ready for me to carve that bird, Pattycake?" he asked. No one but Steve Greene could get away with calling her that.

"Yes, but you have to get out of the way first." She smiled and squeezed past him with another casserole dish, this one full of squash. "Ruth, can you get Grandma Greene's little glass dish for me? I want to put the cranberry sauce in it."

Ruth retrieved the small glass bowl with the tiny leaves etched around the edges from the china cabinet. It was almost never used; the antique was a reminder of the accomplished attorney's inability to win an argument with her mother-in-law.

For the past few Thanksgivings, Ruth had passed up the turkey her mother always roasted. Last year, her mother had heated a frozen vegetarian turkey burger in the microwave and, with great ceremony, placed it atop some dressing on Ruth's plate. This year Ruth told her mother not to bother. "I'm not the purist I used to be," she confessed. "A vegetarian could starve in Indiana."

When the turkey was carved and all three were seated,

Ruth's mother paused. "Well. I have plenty to be thankful for this year."

Ruth started to pass the bread around, but stopped. They had not said grace, at Thanksgiving or any other time, since they stopped going to church.

Her father spread a cloth napkin in his lap, blue eyes glancing from one woman to the other from behind wire-framed glasses he used all the time now, not just to read. Ruth had always thought he would make a great spy, with his thinning shock of brown hair, cardigan sweaters that never quite hung evenly, and cavernous store of political knowledge. "We've got Ruth here," he rumbled.

Her mother nodded. "I'm happy to be here, too." She looked as though she were about to say something else, but changed her mind. "All right, eat up before it gets cold." She seemed different. Her neat, shoulder-length hair had a few more gray strands, perhaps, or maybe she'd taken up aerobics again and lost a few pounds. The whole house somehow felt as if an earthquake or other force had come along and shifted everything just enough to make you wonder what happened — and Ruth sensed her mother was the epicenter.

After they finished dinner and cleaned up, Ruth brewed a pot of decaffeinated gourmet French roast. She could hear what sounded like a football game, or highlights thereof, from the television set in the den. Her father would be in there with at least one book, or some student papers, in his lap, looking up every now and then for the score. Ruth hoped he would like the terra cotta garden gnome, hand-painted by one of her students, she'd bought him for Christmas.

Her mother sat on the deck, feet propped up on another chair. Ruth handed her one of the steaming, fragrant mugs, and they sat together in the dusk.

"I know I haven't seen you for a while," Ruth began, "but something's different." She took a sip of coffee, enjoying its warmth in the cool breeze that rustled the trees in her parents' back yard. "Are you okay?"

"I am now." Her smile faded. "I had breast cancer a few months ago."

Ruth almost dropped her mug. "What?"

"Something turned up on my mammogram in May, probably a week or two before you headed east, and they did a biopsy and told me it had to come out. It was small and contained, so they did a lumpectomy instead of removing the breast altogether."

Again the mug almost fell out of Ruth's hand, and she quickly set it on the table. She fought to tame and organize the words that flooded her mind. "Why in heaven's name didn't you tell me?"

She sighed. "When I found out it was malignant and I'd have to have surgery, you'd already left. When you didn't return my call, I thought about calling you in Indiana... but I couldn't stand the thought of you rushing back here and walking the halls of the hospital. Your dad did enough pacing and fidgeting for both of you, for one thing. Anyway, I decided to wait and see how it went... and then things looked good and there wasn't anything to tell you, really."

"Only that you were all right," Ruth said, a little more sharply than she meant to. She put her head in her hands. "My God. *Are* you all right? Did they get it all — will you—"

"Yes, I'm fine," her mother said. "I didn't need any chemo or radiation. I saw my doctor a couple of weeks ago for follow-up, and she says I'm as good as new. Except for this little dent."

Ruth returned her mother's smirk, but she could not stop a tear or two from rolling down her cheek. "Oh, Mom." She took a breath. "I'm so sorry. I should have called back instead of just leaving a message before I left town. I should have called over the summer. But..."

"Well, I could have called, too."

"Weren't you scared?"

Her own feelings, especially any kind of fear or doubt, were not Ruth's mother's favorite subject. "Yes, I was just about scared out of my mind. I guess we both know that's why I didn't call — that would have made it all the more real." She leaned forward and took Ruth's hand. "I had all kinds of people to talk to and answer my questions — radiologists, oncology nurses, the whole works. A woman from a breast cancer support group even came to my hospital room. Your dad stayed right by my side every minute he could. Lots of clients and colleagues sent cards and came to visit. It was really heartening."

"That's good." Ruth was still reeling from the knowledge that her mother could have died.

"But I realized that the person I most wanted to see and talk to was you." Her eyes were moist behind her bifocals, something else Ruth hadn't seen before.

"And I wasn't there." More tears pressed at the dam.

Her mother squeezed her hand. "I had as much to do with that as you did. The phone works both ways... but I think we should test it more often. Just to make sure." She smiled a little.

"I think so, too." Ruth sniffled.

Her mother brushed away a tear. "Aren't we a pair." She sat back and breathed in the night air. "You haven't said much about your summer in the heartland."

Ruth flexed her shoulders and neck, listening to the trees again. "I miss the bugs that light up the yard at night." She sighed. "You know that dumb song about leaving your heart in San Francisco?"

"That's my native city and my generation, sweetheart. Of course I know it."

"I left mine in Indiana."

"Oh?"

"Belinda. The doctor."

"Now, she is Marina's mother's... help me out here."

"Cousin. Don't ask me if it's once removed or twice removed. Naomi explained it to me, but I can't keep track." Ruth sighed. "I wasn't looking for this, and she wasn't either. I mean, she's older than me and she lives in this little Indiana town where everyone's family has been there for two hundred years and most of the women go by Mrs. Joe Smith or whatever their husband's name is. But things... developed."

Her mother studied her. "This sounds serious."

"I was going to stay out there. I had a job lined up and everything." She fell silent again. "Then Naomi found out, and all hell broke loose. Belinda lost a few patients, and someone threw a brick through her office window. Her daughter freaked out and wouldn't let her see her granddaughter."

Her mother's eyebrows rose. Then she shook her head. "This sounds like a case I had a few years ago. A couple of cases, actually. I imagine Indiana has a very different set of laws. So what did you do then?"

"I couldn't let her go through that." Ruth tapped her foot on the deck, remembering the summer she and her father put it together plank by plank. "So I left."

"Oh, honey. What about her? Did she want you to go?" She narrowed her eyes, and Ruth wondered if a segue from legal eagle to mother bear was in the offing.

"I don't... well, I guess I don't know anymore." Ruth paused. "We've talked on the phone a couple of times since I've been back, but we're so careful with each other. When I hang up it tears my heart out. But I can't go back there and mess things up for her again."

Her mother drank the last of her coffee, her eyes seeming to study the dusk-draped trees. "Ruth, in terms of your having caused the discriminatory treatment Belinda suffered, that's an open-and-shut case — you didn't. What other circumstances have you taken into account?"

"Huh?"

Her mother smiled. "I'm cross-examining, I guess." She

fell silent, then finally asked, "Do you... love her?"

"Yes."

"Does she love you?"

Ruth hesitated. "Yes."

Again her mother said nothing for a while. "Do you think... this is it?"

This time Ruth could not stop the tears; she knew she couldn't and didn't especially want to. Her mother leaned over and stroked Ruth's hair. Ruth grabbed a paper napkin from the ceramic napkin holder and blotted her face, trying to come up for air.

Her mother put both feet on the deck, as if that would help her find the right words. "I wish... that she weren't so far away. This place where she lives doesn't sound like the most open and progressive community in the world, and that frightens me. And it sounds like she's closer to my age than yours." She paused. "All that aside, I think you have to decide where your heart is and what you most value. And then you fight for it, even if you have to fight yourself." The furrowed brow gave way to a gentle smile. "How does that go... where your treasure is, there your heart will be, also?"

Ruth stood up, leaned over, and gave her a kiss on the cheek. "Did they teach you how to argue like this in law school?"

"Nope. Mother school. I did pay attention once or twice."

Ruth picked up the phone on the first ring. "Hello?"

"Hi. I just got home from the book group and got your message. What's up?"

Ruth smiled, warmed by Belinda's voice. "Do you have pen and paper handy?"

"Sure, why?"

"Write this down: Delta Flight 4116 from St. Louis, arriving in Indianapolis at 4:20 p.m. on the twenty-first."

There was a long pause. "Ruth," Belinda began, her voice cooling. "I don't think this is such a good idea. You'll be —"

"I'll be there."

Chapter Twenty-Two

The plane circled Indianapolis, waiting its turn to land. Ruth looked at her watch. She was on time, even if she had lost track of what time zone she was in.

She was lucky to have booked any kind of air travel during the holiday season on such short notice. The agent had paged through heaps of data on his computer screen, finally sending her on a disjointed route from San Francisco to Indianapolis. She had waited for hours in Dallas, dashed through the terminal in Denver and just made her connection, only to face a five-hour layover in St. Louis. And for all she knew, Belinda had a return ticket waiting for her in Indianapolis.

The plane landed with a neat bump. The moment it stopped at the gate, everyone sprang up even though they would have to stand and wait for passengers in front of them to gather their things and file out.

An icy draft seeped through the jet-way and Ruth's denim jacket. She had landed in a state far different from the hot, humid one she had left. This was a cold, gray, and foreign place, possibly with no familiar faces at the end of the jet-way which shook under the footsteps of the bulky family in front of her.

Inside the terminal, a sea of faces and bundled-up forms surrounded the gate. Grandparents and grandchildren squealed, hugged, and kissed their hellos and scores of people hurried past with armloads and bags full of wrapped presents. Ruth stood in the middle of the corridor as bodies swarmed around and past her, some looking twice at her eyebrow ring. She scanned the crowd at the gate, all of it blurring in front of her.

She stopped in her tracks and nearly got rammed from behind by a stroller. There she was, leaning against a railing just past three or four clusters of welcomers and welcomees.

Ruth picked her way around the greeters and travelers. Belinda watched her closely, as if she might be someone else. When Ruth drew closer, the pensive expression turned into a shy smile. Belinda carried a heavy winter coat, not unlike the one she was wearing.

"Somehow, I knew you wouldn't be prepared for this weather." She wrapped the coat around Ruth.

"You'd be surprised." Ruth focused on Belinda's blue eyes. Everything she had wanted to say at this moment escaped her.

Belinda, her hands on the coat's wide lapels, pulled her into a quick embrace. Ruth breathed in the scent of winter.

"Well," Belinda said, "let's go."

Ruth opened her eyes. Certainly she must be on a plane or in an airport somewhere, waiting. But she was on Belinda's living room sofa, where she had crashed almost as soon as they arrived.

Neither of them had said much on the drive from Indianapolis. There was catching-up chitchat, talk about the weather — a few inches of snow blanketed the ground — and a delicate dance around anything more substantial.

Ruth sat up and stretched. A small artificial Christmas

NANCY CROWE

tree stood on the end table, complete with tiny lights and an assortment of ornaments, including a felt Santa Claus from one of Sarah's Sunday school classes and a ceramic angel Eliza had made long ago. Aside from the tree and a lone, unlighted bayberry candle on the dining room windowsill, that was the extent of Belinda's holiday decorating. Almost every other house on the block was bedecked with lights, angels, or illuminated plastic manger scenes, and some had all three. Lula had placed candles — the kind whose glow came from a switch rather than a wick, but candles nevertheless — in every window of her house.

Belinda sat at her makeshift end-of-the-table desk in the dining room, using the electric typewriter to fill out a form. She looked up, and the air crackled between them.

"How long was I asleep?"

Belinda took off her glasses and smiled, holding Ruth's gaze. "A couple of hours. I had a feeling you'd be tired after that long trip." She pulled her gaze from Ruth to the paper in front of her. "Are you hungry? I have some leftover casserole I can heat up. I wasn't sure how off-track your eating schedule would be, so I didn't plan anything, but I can have this ready in just a little bit." She was out of the chair and into the kitchen by the time she had finished the sentence.

Ruth freshened up in the half bath downstairs, splashing cold water on her face. Rather than face the awkward question of where to take her suitcase upstairs, she had left it by the front door.

After dinner, they took their tea into the living room. Belinda settled into the easy chair, and Ruth sat in a corner of the sofa. A minute or two of silence passed; they had spent all of their small talk tokens.

"You want to tell me why you're here?" Belinda asked.

"Because I want to be here."

Belinda sighed. "It's not that I'm not happy to see you... I am. But I'm not sure what you're expecting to happen. You made your choice and went back to San Francisco, which you had every reason to do." She laced her fingers together in her lap. "I think it's best if we let it go."

Ruth's heart began to sink. "What exactly do you mean?"

"We have to be honest with ourselves. There's the age difference. Then there's my family and this town." Belinda set her cup on the end table. "Jan's new venture seems to be going all right, as far as I know, but if that didn't work out, you wouldn't be able to get a job here."

Ruth felt the blood drain from her face. She knew this would happen. "Where's the crystal ball that's telling you all this?" she asked, careful to keep her voice even.

"Ruth, I don't need a crystal ball. I have almost fifty years of experience living in this place and living with myself. It just leads to more pain if you step out of your… reach. I wish I could make you understand that."

Ruth examined her nails. She'd been an idiot to come here, and now she had to gather what was left of her dignity. Belinda was right; you could only go so far. The sooner you learned that, the sooner you grew up and had to explain it to those who didn't know any better.

"I do understand," she said. "I understand now, anyway." She rose from the sofa. "I'll get on a standby list for the next flight west. Or I'll take a bus."

Belinda leaned against the arm of her chair, rubbing her eyes and temples. When she spoke again, Ruth could barely hear her. "I think that's best."

Ruth lay awake past midnight in the catch-all room. Although she had cried until her ribs ached, she had not worn herself out enough to sleep.

She got up and padded downstairs in her sweats. The furnace switched off with a series of twittering creaks, and the floor chilled her feet even through the thick socks. How did anyone survive in this cold that came in anywhere it could find?

No more tea. She walked into the dark living room, arms folded across her chest. She switched on the brass lamp in the corner, the family hand-me-down that Mark had rewired for Belinda, and looked around. A fine coating of dust covered the family photographs on the mantel; nothing had been added or subtracted since August. Except for the Christmas tree and a different assortment of medical journals scattered across the coffee table, the room looked the same.

Ruth sank into the sofa and drew herself into a tight ball. It was so God-damned pathetic, shivering in the middle of the night after flying two thousand miles to be with someone who didn't want her. After promising that they would work through the complications, Belinda had decided that Ruth wasn't worth the effort, and maybe she wasn't.

"No!"

She got to her feet and paced, careful not to creak the floorboards and not sure if she cared anyway. She wanted to yell. Scream. Break something. Every muscle tightened like armor as she kept walking, trying to keep from taking a swing at the Christmas tree. If Belinda came downstairs, she would get a withering earful.

Ruth's eye fell upon a small Bible at the end of one of the built-in bookshelves, dwarfed beside an old medical dictionary. She drew it out and opened the cover. It was a standard-issue Sunday school Bible from Belinda's church, given to her when she was about ten. Ruth flipped through the pages to where the red ribbon marked the beginning of the Psalms.

She curled up in the easy chair. Beginning with Psalm 1, she read each one, all the way to the last line of Psalm 150, and her breathing fell into an even rhythm. *Truly, I am like one who does not hear, and in whose mouth is no retort.*

As a child, she had wondered if these ancient songsters

were for real; now she decided they had to be. At some point, those who called themselves people of God had to be real.

NANCY CROWE

Chapter Twenty-Three

Ruth extricated a bottle of water from the rack in the convenience store refrigerator. It seemed silly to drink cold water when the air outside was so bitter, but her mouth felt like burlap and the borrowed winter coat hung on her like full body armor. Outside, Joey, the gas station attendant she'd mistaken for a would-be murderer, cleaned the windows of a white Oldsmobile tinged a grayish brown from the slush and exhaust. Belinda had had a neighbor drop her off at the office and let Ruth borrow her car for whatever travel-related errands she needed to run, and Ruth had decided the first order of business was to fill the tank.

She found Jim Foster in line at the counter with a package of Oreos.

"Hi, Jim."

He turned around, and his eyes went wide behind the dark-rimmed glasses. "Ruth Greene, as I live and breathe," he said, pulling her into a big bear hug. "You've come back to us in time for Christmas."

"I couldn't miss your Christmas Eve service," she said, smiling.

"Well, now I have extra motivation to get that sermon

written." He reached under his own heavy coat for his wallet and paid for the cookies. "The one vice I have left," he said as he picked up the bag.

"I won't tell the elders," Ruth said.

He laughed. "Listen, Jan's agency is doing great, but I'm sure she could still use your help. Come see us, all right? Oh…" He turned around at the door. "I meant to call her myself, but could you remind Belinda about that Sunday school class she's supposed to start leading next month? I want to make sure we're on her calendar."

Sunday school? "Will do." She stared after him as the cashier rang up her bottled water, and almost forgot her change. She hurried back outside and into the car before the cold air could reach too far into her consciousness.

Ruth drove around the square. Thankfully, most of the snow had been salted away or plowed from the roads, but the white stuff still covered the ground, clothed the bare branches of trees, and bunched up uncomfortably along the streets. Snow changed the town; its whiteness evened things out, especially on a cloudy day. New Bethlehem never really rushed, except maybe when the factory's first shift let out, but a kind of rush-hour energy propelled people up and down the sidewalks. You couldn't do any real shopping downtown anymore, Naomi had said; just odds and ends. Ruth supposed the demand for odds and ends rose dramatically three days before Christmas.

She checked the address she had copied from New Bethlehem's thin new phone book and parked behind the familiar small car, which still bore a California license plate. The two-story frame house at 704 Blanton had seen better days but still had some kick left; the other cars parked up and down the street were a hodgepodge of junk heaps, pickup trucks, and marginally respectable sedans. A creaky, wooden flight of stairs along the side of the house led up to 704-B. That had to be hard on Naomi's knee.

NANCY CROWE

Naomi looked smaller, but maybe it was because she was bundled up in a thick turtleneck with a pink sweater thrown over it. She did not seem particularly surprised to see Ruth at her door. "Heard you were in town." She looked at Ruth, past her, then down at the Welcome Friends mat she'd kept outside on Estancia Boulevard.

"How? I just got in yesterday."

"Sissy Wallace saw you and Belinda drive by while she was out trying to fix one of her Christmas lights. Gawkin' at you probably kept her from electrocuting herself."

"Is she the one who lives over on Fourth and hung her laundry out to dry when it was real windy?"

"That's the one. Her unmentionables ended up in the Baptist preacher's front yard."

Ruth couldn't help smiling. Then her mouth tightened. "May I come in?"

Naomi, too, turned serious again. "I reckon you better. It's colder than heck out there." She stepped to one side. Her thick white socks made the maroon house slippers look painfully small.

Naomi had managed to squeeze everything from her old apartment, which wasn't exactly spacious, into this tiny abode. She had everything arranged pretty much the same way, except you couldn't walk more than a few steps without bumping into something. Ruth took a nearby chair and Naomi sat on the edge of the sofa. She did not look at Ruth.

"When Marina left, I had a lot of trouble understanding why," Ruth began. "I know you did, too. But I'm having even more trouble understanding why you found it necessary to talk about Belinda and me all over town."

Naomi's face flushed, and her jaw clenched the way Marina's had when Ruth confronted her. "I didn't talk about anybody all over town. You must've heard wrong," she said huskily.

A lump the size of a golf ball formed in Ruth's throat, but

she could not let it choke her. "You know I'm not stupid enough to believe that. And I know you're smart enough to understand the harm you've done." She saw that her own fists were clenched and spread her hands flat on her knees. "I don't care what you believe about what's right and wrong or if you think I'm the devil incarnate. You had no right to do that."

"Well, I was just beside myself after... seeing what I saw." Naomi reddened.

"I wasn't the picture of calm myself after you barged in on us like that."

"Barged in? Why, I..." She got up and walked into the kitchen, her back to Ruth. "What the hell are you doing here, anyway?"

"I came back because I love Belinda," Ruth said.

Naomi said nothing, but her shoulders tensed under the thin pink sweater, the one she had pulled around her against the Nevada roadside winds. She picked up a dish on the counter, then shoved it aside.

"Don't you get it? I came here in the first place because I was concerned about you. You were just about flattened emotionally when we left San Francisco. Even when we got here, you wouldn't talk to me, you wouldn't talk to Belinda, and you wouldn't hardly move out of the living room chair to say hello to people who have known you your whole damn life. Then you spent some time with your old friends, and with Sarah, and you and I finally got to know each other." Ruth caught her breath. "Then you put yourself in the wrong place at the wrong time and didn't have the decency to mind your own business, and it tore people apart — people you supposedly cared about. Does that make you happy? Does it make up for everything you've lost?"

Naomi turned her head. "You got no call to talk to me like that."

"I have every call to tell you how angry I am."

Neither of them moved, and after a minute or two of silence Ruth stood up. "I have to go." She shrugged back into her coat.

Naomi did not turn from the kitchen counter. "Better get you a hat," she said as Ruth opened the door. "It's freezing out there, and you'll lose heat out of that hot head of yours."

It was the first time anyone had accused Ruth of having a hot head. She decided to take it as a compliment.

❧

Silver garlands lined the front window of *Cover the World*. Will, wearing a red and green argyle sweater and pants that actually looked as if they had been pressed, chatted with a young couple in the travel section, gesturing with a book in his hand. When Ruth came in, he handed the book to the man and moved to greet her.

"Well, if it isn't the ghost of Christmas present!" He vigorously shook her hand. "I thought you'd disappeared back into the wilds of the West, never to be heard from again. Have you eaten?"

He did not wait for an answer. In less than thirty seconds he had grabbed his coat, yelled to the clerk that he was going to lunch, and was ushering Ruth down the street. "You have to try Richie's new grilled veggie sandwich. I never thought something like that would fly in this community of carnivores, but he says it's selling."

Ruth struggled to keep up. She listened to Will talk about the appalling eating habits of Frank's son, who was staying with them over Christmas break; his rather sluggish holiday sales season; and, of course, the weather, until they were seated at a window table at Richie's. The diner looked exactly the same except for the red and white stockings, one for each employee with the names in glitter-covered glue, hanging on the wall behind the counter.

"Okay, Will." She held up her hands. "That's all very interesting, but I need you to tell me what's going on around here. No embellishments, no tangents — just the truth."

He seemed taken aback and fell silent for a few seconds. "So what do you want to know?"

"I want to know what kind of flak Belinda is getting. How many patients does she have left? Has there been any more vandalism, or harassment? Is —"

"Who do I look like, the Secret Service? Coffee, please, Richie, and I believe we'll have two of your veggie specials. If that's all right with Ruth, that is," he added in mock solicitousness.

She nodded. "That's fine. How've you been, Richie?"

He stood there in his smudged apron, glancing from one to the other and looking as if he'd forgotten part of a large order. "Well, I'm ready for Santy Claus to bring me a nice long vacation. You forget something last summer and come back for it?"

"You might say that." She smiled. After he left, she turned back to Will. "No, you're not the Secret Service, but you'll have to do. What's up?"

"Oh, you know New Bethlehem. Nothing much happens here, or happens any different than it happened before." He sighed heavily and leaned back in his chair, the hint of a smirk showing behind the beard.

Now she'd have to work to get information out of him, and he'd enjoy every minute of it. "What about Belinda's practice?" she asked, as patiently as she could manage.

"Oh, I suppose she's doing all right. I see cars outside the office all the time. One of my friends over in Waynesville, a teacher who's one of the girls, got sick of her doctor asking about birth control and decided to start seeing Belinda instead, despite the thirty-minute drive. And, let's see, there was a woman who came into the store and asked where she could find 'that doctor.'" He wiggled his fingers to make quote marks. "Seems she had a teenage daughter with some serious shit going on and thought maybe the kid would talk to this doctor. I really ought to get a cut for these referrals, don't you think?"

"Patients are seeking Belinda out?"

"Well, I'm not her receptionist. In fact, I haven't seen much of the good doctor since she came in a couple of weeks ago with her daughter and that annoyingly mobile child. She's going to have her hands full with another one on the way. I swear, I'd rather —"

"Hold it!" Ruth said, a little louder than she intended. "Belinda and Eliza and Sarah all came in together?" He nodded. "And Eliza's pregnant?"

"Either that or something else is making her look fat and peaked. You didn't know?"

"No." She sat there, hands flat on the table. "I didn't know. Did they... seem to be getting along?"

He shrugged. "I guess."

Richie brought their sandwiches — grilled peppers, onions, tomatoes, and zucchini with a drizzle of cheese on Italian bread. It was probably delicious, and Richie probably deserved a compliment, but Ruth barely noticed. As Will rattled on to the next topic and the one after that, a wild joy, infused with anger, steeped in her chest.

They walked back in the cold, and Ruth headed for the car. She looked at her watch; the meal she and Will had just eaten was more of an early dinner than a late lunch. It was almost five o'clock. There was something she needed to do, and quickly.

Chapter Twenty-Four

Naomi switched on another light in the apartment; it wasn't even six yet and dark as midnight outside.

On the record spinning on her stereo, the gospel quartet sang about an unbroken circle. Marina and Cara had wanted to get her one of those disc players for years, but all her favorites were either on tape or in the record albums she kept in their cardboard jackets in the cabinet. She even had a few eight-tracks somewhere.

The landlord would have to do something about her windows; cold drafts sneaked in all over the place and wrapped themselves around her neck and shoulders. Or maybe it was that blast of cold air Ruth brought when she'd come in and lit into Naomi. That girl had some nerve.

She sat down at the kitchen table, which was in the living room, with the basket of Christmas cards she'd received. Many had been forwarded twice. Naomi had sent cards only to people she knew would take offense if they didn't get a card from her, and had simply signed her name. She didn't feel like explaining the change of address or scribbling cheery little notes about the past year.

Cara had not written or called, and Naomi tried to stop

hoping she would. Every day she wanted to haul out the phone book and hire a private eye or call information for every city and cow town in Texas, just to know where Cara was. Then she could hatch a plan to get her back, to offer some irresistible gesture or gem of motherly wisdom. It would do no good, because her younger daughter knew something she didn't. She knew what it meant to lose a child, to know that her son's body was in the ground and his soul was somewhere she could not reach or even imagine. Cara could not search for baby Evan; she couldn't hope that he would come to his senses and return to her.

For Marina, there was an address. A real street address in her daughter's handwriting, in the upper left corner of the red envelope. Naomi had read the Christmas card when it arrived two days ago; it had a generic manger scene on the front and a printed greeting and a scribbled "Marina" inside. For two days it had sat, untouched, beside the Christmas card basket.

Naomi took out a pen and a blank Christmas card; the chances of any mail making its way to Seattle by Christmas were slim to none, but she didn't care.

Ruth had talked as if Naomi had set out to crucify her and Belinda. If she felt that way, why had she come back for more? You didn't fly all that way during the holidays unless you were pretty sure it would be worth the trip. Naomi remembered Ruth and Belinda coming home from the office together, fixing supper, and sitting with her while she watched television. Why had Naomi never seen Ruth so at ease as she was in New Bethlehem, a place that must have been as foreign to her as San Francisco had been to Naomi? Belinda had a way about her when Ruth was around, as if someone had given her a gift she didn't expect. But Ruth was the one who'd returned; she had bought a ticket she probably couldn't afford, left that place where there were thousands like her, and had come back to New Bethlehem.

After twenty minutes of staring at nothing, Naomi put down the pen and went to the kitchen drawer where she kept the phone book and a big file folder full of recipes she'd cut out over the years but never tried. It was so much easier to find things in the New Bethlehem phone book, and it didn't hurt your hands to pick it up. Advertising, Air Conditioning, Airlines. She picked up the phone and dialed the toll-free number.

Maybe Marina had found someone else out there in Seattle. It was nothing she'd ever tell Naomi about. She had no idea if Marina was happy, and maybe she never had. If she flew to Seattle and had a cab take her to the address on that envelope, God only knew if Marina would let her in or if she would blame Marina if she didn't. She hadn't been there for Marina; why would Marina believe she would be now? The automated voice came on the line and thanked her for calling, but Naomi hung up and edged around the table to the stereo.

"Sorry, fellas." She lifted the needle and brought the turntable to a stop. In the rack where she kept her cassettes, she found the Indigo Girls tape Ruth had left in the car after they drove out from San Francisco. She popped it in and pushed the button. Marina liked their music, too.

Naomi sat back down and listened to the Indigo Girls sing. She thought of Ruth humming along with that same music as they drove east, of Marina carrying an umbrella — she heard it rained a lot in Seattle — as she went about her separate life there, of Cara beaming as she placed little Evan in his grandma's arms, of Belinda bringing a hot cup of coffee upstairs to her when she first returned to her home town. She thought of her own mother, brewing coffee in the kitchen while her father stumbled in the front door and Naomi hurried her brother and sisters out the back. God had scattered them, dropped each woman into a life she'd have to figure out as she went along, and left them to look for one another.

NANCY CROWE

Naomi took a deep breath. She would make the trip to Seattle. She'd take as many planes as she had to to get there, and when she did she'd have a taxi deliver her to Marina's door. She would make two cups of hot cocoa from scratch the way she did when the girls were little, sit down in Marina's kitchen or living room, and listen to her talk about her job or her friends or whatever else she wanted to talk about. She would listen without interrupting, all night if Marina wanted. Then, perhaps, Naomi could rest.

But first, she would call. She flipped the phone book back to the front, found the area code, and dialed. "Seattle, please... Bittner, B-i-t-t-n-e-r... Marina, but it might be just M. The address is — yes, thank you." She wrote the number on the back of a grocery receipt, hung up, and had to sit down again. For several minutes she sat there, staring at the scribbled sequence of numbers and watching them blur.

Naomi grabbed for a tissue, wiped her eyes, and tried to focus on the music. She might not understand, but she'd better listen.

After two more songs, a few deep breaths, and a silent but pointed prayer, she picked up the phone.

Chapter Twenty-Five

Something had blown up in the kitchen. There was no other explanation for the bowls, cookie sheets, measuring cups, containers, and traces of flour and what looked like cinnamon or nutmeg covering every level surface. From the doorway, Ruth watched Belinda read from a cookbook while she stirred something in a large metal mixing bowl.

"Hi."

Belinda froze, then turned around. "Hi."

Ruth hung up the heavy coat and went to the sink to wash her hands. She found another open cookbook, assessed the nearby ingredients to determine which dish was under construction, and began to slice a yam.

Belinda stirred some more and adjusted the oven. Then she frowned, set the large spoon aside, and reached for the hand mixer. Its whine filled the room.

"It looks like you're expecting company," Ruth said after Belinda switched off the mixer.

She did not turn around. "Eliza and Mark might come over Christmas Eve. I'm trying to put a few things together ahead of time."

Ruth forced her voice to stay calm. "So you and Eliza are

working things out?"

"Maybe." Belinda shrugged.

Oh, this Midwestern reserve. "That's good. Especially with another grandchild on the way."

Belinda stopped stirring and turned around. "How on earth do you know that?"

"That's just one of the things I know. There's also the fact that you and Eliza and Sarah were in Will's store together. And the patients who are coming to you not in spite of who you are, but because of it. And then there's that Sunday school class you're leading; Jim wanted me to remind you about that." Ruth put down the knife and walked toward her, holding her gaze. "Did you forget to tell me these things, or did you not see them yourself?"

Belinda's face turned as pale as the snow outside. "I thought I mentioned some of that earlier. Anyway," she said, pouring half a cup of nuts and stirring it into the mixture, "did you get a ticket back?"

Ruth placed both hands on the counter behind her. "I'm not going anywhere."

Belinda whirled around, knocking the mixing bowl out of her hands and onto the floor with a muffled clunk. "You — what?" She stooped to pick up the bowl; the dough was thick enough that none of it had spilled out.

Ruth grabbed the bowl with one hand and Belinda's hand with the other. She pulled Belinda to her feet and set the bowl on the counter. "You heard me."

"But... Ruth, we already discussed this." Belinda's face was flushed.

"That was a sorry excuse for a discussion if you weren't telling me the truth."

"Who told you all this?" Belinda backed away, one hand on her hip.

"Will, mostly."

"That blowhard," she hissed.

"Maybe, but did he tell me anything that wasn't true?"

Belinda wiped some flour off her hands and threw the towel onto the counter. "No."

"Then what the hell is going on?"

Belinda took a deep breath and let it out in a long sigh. She flipped a few pages in a cookbook, put away a box of baking soda, and rinsed and dried a measuring cup. "It's one thing to have everything falling apart around you," she said finally. "You're alone, and you know it. It's kind of like when I was a resident at University Hospital... when you have multiple traumas coming in on top of what you've already got, there's no question about what you're supposed to do. You save the ones you can and try to comfort the ones left behind when you can't. You try not to think about it more than you have to, let alone feel, but you know that if you stop caring you might as well quit." She walked from one end of the kitchen to another, catching her breath. "When everyone loves you and trusts you and expects only the best from you... and I'm not necessarily talking about the hospital any more." She swallowed hard.

"I know," Ruth said quietly.

"That's when you have to watch out — because that's when you'll be found lacking. That's when someone will touch you in such a way that you can't maintain the illusion of being someone who has all the answers, or even some of the answers, and discover that you're just... yourself." Belinda leaned against the counter.

Ruth edged closer to Belinda. "I like yourself better than any answer you could come up with," she said. Belinda did not look at her, and she waited a moment or two. "Have you and Eliza come to any kind of understanding?" she asked finally.

"Does an unspoken agreement not to talk about the issue count as understanding?" Belinda sighed. "When Griff and I separated, Eliza was furious. She blamed him for everything and wouldn't talk to him on the phone or visit him. I knew forcing her to do so would backfire, and Griff... well, he just kept trying. After a while she realized he was still there, he was still her father, and he still loved her." Sadness, not without hope, loomed in Belinda's eyes. "I suppose it could be the same with me, now. After all, Eliza and I have both grown up a bit since then." She smiled a little.

"She might be angrier now than she was last summer," Ruth said as gently as she could. "She might keep you from Sarah again — and the new baby."

"I know." Belinda's voice caught, and tears filled her eyes. "But I'm still here, I'm still her mother, and I still love her. And I know I can't do a damn thing more than that."

"If this town can grow in its own quirky ways, your family can too." Ruth took Belinda's hand again. "But what I care about is you. Not what you can do or who you can please. Just you."

"Ruth, you don't know..." She paused. "I've lived in the same town for almost all of my life, but I've been running for years. From myself, mostly. And you..." She let go and began to pace again, then turned to face Ruth. "You made it so difficult for me to keep running, and the funny thing was that I didn't really want to anymore. Maybe that scared me as much as everything else that happened. So I closed myself down until I couldn't see what was right in front of me — most of all, you. And now here you are, and I can barely stand to walk around my own damn kitchen, let alone run anywhere." One tear, then another, coursed down her cheek.

"We might have to leave New Bethlehem. I know that," Ruth said quietly. "We might want to leave. Or we might want to stay." She met Belinda in the center of the kitchen and clasped both her hands. "Wherever you go, I will go."

Belinda's face was a slate of jumbled questions, just as it had been that first day in the office, when she stepped out of her reach and toward Ruth. Then, as if she had been up all night wrestling with a complex scientific problem and discovered the solution in her own scribbled notes, her blue eyes cleared, took Ruth in, and held her. Ruth waited, hearing only their breathing and the soft creaks of the house settling around them.

Belinda grasped Ruth's hands and pulled them toward her heart. Her voice returned, clear like her eyes. "And I'll go with you."

Ruth felt tears pool in her own eyes. She held out her arms, but Belinda was already there.

When night had fallen, Ruth joined Belinda at the dining room window. They stood together in the dark, looking out at multicolored blinking bulbs outlining the house across the street and wiry angels guarding the lawn two doors down, all of it illuminating rooftops and trees against snow and sky.

"I really should have put up some lights." Belinda sighed.

Ruth laid a warm, steady hand on Belinda's shoulder. She reached into one of the china cabinet drawers for the matches they used to start the grill in the summer. She moved the bayberry candle closer to the window and, in one smooth motion, set it ablaze.

NANCY CROWE

About the author

Nancy Crowe, a graduate of Louisville Seminary, has spent much of her career as a newspaper copy editor and freelance writer. She lives in Indiana with her partner and their cat and dog.

Fine lesbian books from

ODD GIRLS PRESS
P. O. Box 2157, Anaheim CA 92814-0157
800-821-0632 email: publisher@oddgirlspress.com
web: www.oddgirlspress.com

Bethlehem Road by Nancy Crowe. Naomi Bittner, returning to her roots in the Midwest, is unhappy that Ruth Greene, the discarded girlfriend of her daughter, Marina, has insisted on accompanying her. As Ruth wends her way through the small town life, she uncovers secrets, and closets. One of those closets is occupied by the highly admired town doctor, Belinda Boaz. An attraction building between Belinda and Ruth seems to have a hopeless future: Belinda is a generation removed from Ruth in age, and has a daughter and grandchildren. Then, suddenly, events careen out of control in the town of New Bethlehem. 1-887237-00-3 $12.95

Monologues and Scenes for Lesbian Actors by Carolyn Gage. Finally! A book for lesbians who are tired of "passing" at auditions and in acting classes and workshops! Here at last, from one of the most talented and inventive contemporary playwrights, is a book of twenty-five monologues and forty-five scenes by, for, and about lesbians. 1-887237-10-0 $15.95 trade paper.

Pelt by Daphne Gottlieb. Using the language of the everyday to express the extraordinary, poet Daphne Gottlieb searches for the truths of human experience and finds those truths in relationships, childhood, and a woman on fire. From preying to praying, the loss of innocence and the innocence of loss, and the most cruel and unusual stuff of all — love — these poems represent a strong, fresh voice in contemporary poetry. 1-887237-09-7 $9 trade paper.

Gaslight by Carol Guess. Carol Guess has composed, from glass-edged fragments of her life and her work as a creative artist, the mosaic of a woman who has fought to be her true self. *Gaslight* speaks to the expressive individual you have struggled to become. To the questing child and adolescent you once were. Like no other book, *Gaslight* shares each step of the interior process of creation and of failing to create: the process of becoming a writer. In this extraordinary and unforgettable work, Carol Guess brilliantly illuminates the path to art and to individuality. 1-887237-05-4 $15.99 trade paper

First Resort by Nanci Little. Jordan Bryant maintains an almost clinical distance between herself and the people she meets at Catawamteak, the grand resort on the coast of Maine where she is Director of Golf . . . until she meets Gillian Benson. *First Resort* is a meticulous exploration of the growth of the bonds of affection, love, & friendship between women.1-887237-01-1 $11 trade paper.

Night Mare by Franci McMahon. Jane Scott has been investigating a cruel scandal in her world, the theft and/or killing of prized horses for their insurance value. When she accompanies her best friend to evaluate an Arabian horse, Jane knows its price is too cheap — way too cheap. Suddenly, shockingly, Jane is embroiled in a devastating murder — for which she blames herself. A murder that hurls her into the orbit of a beautiful, wild-spirited mare named Night. A murder that will take her to Montana, and to the ranch of a singular woman who holds the power to penetrate every border of Jane's well-guarded, grieving self. 1-887237-14-3 $13 trade paper

Bloodsong by Karen Marie Christa Minns. In lyric and erotic prose, Minns continues the story of the vampire Darsen, first introduced in her Lammy-nominated **Virago**. Against her will, Ginny has been given the bite that is transforming her into a vampire. As Darsen waits for her victim to weaken, Ginny's lover Manilla readies herself for the confrontation when Darsen returns to claim Ginny forever. 1-887237-08-9 $12.95 trade paper.

Tory's Tuesday by Linda Kay Silva. Captured by Nazis while trying to flee Poland, Marissa and Elsa are shipped to the Auschwitz concentration camp, where they are separated. Through the atrocities and horrors both women face, their love for each other never wavers. They meet other courageous women who help them in their fight to survive and reunite. 1-887237-02-X $12.95 trade paper.

ORDERING Our books are available at feminist bookstores, gay and lesbian bookstores, and some independent bookstores and mail-order services. If the book you are looking for is not in stock, the store will order it for you. To order directly from Odd Girls Press please send a list of titles you want and a check for the total + $3.00 to cover shipping charges (Canada $5.00, all other countries 15% of the total cost of books being ordered)

SUBMISSIONS We're always looking for new works. For submission guidelines send a self-addressed stamped envelope to Odd Girls Press or go to our web site and see the Submissions Guidelines web page.